Praise for Melissa Lopez's *Dark Sentinel*

"Intriguing and imaginative, Dark Sentinel is a great read!"

~ Award winning author Bianca D'Arc

"The plot flows seemlessly. The story is hot, fast paced, and reads easily. Time will completely slip away from you as you emerage into the world of this story."

~ Amy Parker, ParaNormalRomance.org

"Dark Sentinel is an outstanding story. The macabre world Melissa Lopez has created is gripping and intriguing."

~ Nannette, Joyfully Reviewed

"Whether you believe in an afterlife, purgatory, or even hell doesn't matter; this makes a very interesting story. Dark Sentinel is book one of a series of books about the Netherworld and it is a very good start. I will definitely be reading the next one to see what will happen next!"

~ Steph B., The Romance Studio

"The emotions are keen and real, the sex is hot, and the plot is original. I would rec it in a heartbeat!"

~ Nicole Grissom, MyBookstoreAndMore.com

"I've never read a book by this author before but after reading this book I only want more."

~ *Laetitia, I Read Romance So What?*

"This book is like a piece of cheesecake, thick, rich and sinful. [...] This book is a very quick and passionate read that will have you squirming. It was very enjoyable and I look forward to reading any future offerings from Ms. Lopez."

~ *T.S. Peters, JERR*

"The couple is sympathetic, and Lopez maintains the sexual tension between them."

~ *Gail Pruszkowski, Romantic Times BOOKreviews*

"Melissa Lopez has a gifted and fertile imagination. There are no cliches and same-old same-old paranormal plot devices in Dark Sentinel..."

~ *Shannon C., The Good, The Bad and The Unread*

Look for these titles by *Melissa Lopez*

Now Available:

The Thorn Series
Boomerang Love (Book 1)
Riptide Love (Book 2)
True Blue Love (Book 3)

A Story of Netherworld
Dark Sentinel
Dark Chance (Absolution~Book 1)

Dark Sentinel

Melissa Lopez

A Samhain Publishing, Ltd. publication.

Samhain Publishing, Ltd.
577 Mulberry Street, Suite 1520
Macon, GA 31201
www.samhainpublishing.com

Dark Sentinel
Copyright © 2009 by Melissa Lopez
Print ISBN: 978-1-60504-055-4
Digital ISBN: 1-59998-893-3

Editing by Eve Joyce
Cover by Anne Cain

This book is a work of fiction. The names, characters, places, and incidents are products of the writer's imagination or have been used fictitiously and are not to be construed as real. Any resemblance to persons, living or dead, actual events, locale or organizations is entirely coincidental.

All Rights Are Reserved. No part of this book may be used or reproduced in any manner whatsoever without written permission, except in the case of brief quotations embodied in critical articles and reviews.

First Samhain Publishing, Ltd. electronic publication: March 2008
First Samhain Publishing, Ltd. print publication: January 2009

Dedication

Christina Brashear, for allowing me to ramble on about Netherworld and for giving me a chance at seeing my world come to life.

Eve Joyce, for all your support and sharing your knowledge.

Mechele Armstrong, for being the best critique partner ever.

Chapter One

Lash landed on the ground with a bone-jarring thud, bouncing until he slammed against an immovable object. Even if he could, he dared not move. What new form of torture had his keepers invented to use on him? Until that moment, he'd been able to ignore pain. It'd been centuries—no, eons—since he'd felt any emotions or sensations at all, except pain, so he had built up a resistance to the physical reaction. At this moment, the shock of it was a stark reality.

He moaned, fighting the agony. In his existence in Netherworld, he'd known every type of severe abuse fitting for his kind. But never had he felt such suffering. Every bone in his body must have shattered. Too much pain assailed him for them not to be.

He drew in another agonizing breath. Sleep. He willed sleep to claim him. He'd never escape the continual cruelties heaped on him, yet thankfully he'd heal in the slumber of nightmares.

"Hello. Hello. Can you hear me?" The whispered melody reached him from a great distance.

He attempted to growl. He knew this trick well. His keepers tortured the legions relentlessly with promise of concern, of care, only to rip it away.

"Shhh... You've got some nasty bruises." Gentle hands eased him. "Lie still, I'll go get my jeep. I'll take you to a hospital."

He forced his eyes open, only to squeeze them shut against the blinding light. The world he existed in was a gloomy place without such brightness. Yet even at his age he'd not seen all of Netherworld. Through his eyelids the light caused discomfort. Still it was the least of the pain racking his body.

He groaned, deep in his chest. Soft hands skimmed across a torso that couldn't possibly belong to him. His hide had long ago lost all sensitivity. But this gentle touch had him shivering, in a way he'd never responded to the harshest of touches.

"My name is Teva Gibson. I'll do what I can to help you." Her voice was a whisper as if she confided in him. Though running a race couldn't have made her sound more breathless.

He trembled. He'd been wrong. His keepers had found a new form of torture. They'd sent a human female with soft skin and a delicate scent to him. *No.* It had to be a disguise. Which tormentor was it this time? Was she Belial or one of her horde? His breathing turned ragged. It could be any of the keepers. The demon lords were all devious, cunning, beyond redemption.

Lash swallowed past the lump forming in his throat. When was the last time he'd smelled anything other than the putrid bowels of darkness? It was a darkness filled with every vile form of degradation, filth, and every sin imaginable. Not for a very long time, that was for sure.

"Leave me," he snarled half-heartedly, only to moan. He didn't want her to leave, even though her retribution would be fierce.

"Shhh...lie still. I don't want to leave you..."

He inhaled deeply, hoping to catch a whiff of his keepers. Any moment now, she'd rake her claws down his chest, or taunt his cock. The game never stopped for legion lords.

Panic edged her voice. "What happened to you?"

Sweat beaded his upper lip as he waited. He feared breathing, much less speaking to her. If he answered wrong, his punishment would be worse. Much worse

Soft hands caressed his shoulder and brow. "Just hang on. I'll be back."

At the sound of her disappearing footsteps, he rolled over, pushing up onto his hands and knees. He kept his eyes closed, but it did no good; the dizziness came anyway. His world spun, tilting as his stomach rolled. Groaning, he collapsed.

Teva's mind was awhirl with the possibilities of what could have happened to the stranger. While apparently weak from his injuries, there'd been something dangerous about him—something more than his breathtaking masculinity. He had a hardness that stole from his dark male perfection. Coal-black hair with eyes that matched and a jaw darkened by a shadow of growth. And what a jaw line!

Then there was the rest of him... She swallowed, her body heating.

Nude.

Not likely she'd ever forget him lying there naked. Ridges and tight muscles sculpted him from face to foot. God, she'd even noticed his feet. Huge feet. Heat spread along her cheeks. *Yes, Teva, you noticed that, too.* His cock had been long, thick and flaccid between his muscular thighs.

Teva gritted her teeth as the jeep jolted over low rocks. She lived on a privately owned park and wetland preserve in Louisiana, northeast of New Orleans. The Bayou area—a melting pot—drew all types of people. People like her, who tried to hide from the rest of the world. In the tradition of her forefathers.

How did he get out here?

A chill crawled up her spine, setting her hair on edge as she pushed the legends the swamps were famous for from her mind. They were old wives' tales, nothing more. She focused on the more likely possibilities as she urged the four-wheeler forward.

Naked, he didn't look like a hunter. Occasionally they poached on her land. They wanted to brag about bagging an alligator or black bear and get a trophy to take home to mount on their wall. Even nude, the stranger had seemed too clean for it, but what if he was an escaped convict? She'd often heard stories passed down of prisoners running for the shelter of the Bayou. Many of them never to be seen again after falling victim to the mysteries of the swamp. Gators and the dark, brackish water had never been friendly to those who didn't respect them. Perhaps he was a victim of a kidnapping?

She shook her head to turn her thoughts away from the stranger. How he'd gotten out here didn't matter. She had to help him. She concentrated on maneuvering the jeep around marshy areas until she reached the stranger's side.

Killing the engine, she released a relieved breath. She'd worried she'd imagined him. Another part of her wished she had. Her life would be easier. He'd moved while she'd been gone. He now lay face down. Her gaze lingered on the rounded curve of his butt. She bet it would look as fine in clothes as out.

Don't ogle an unconscious man!

Teva shivered as another chill raced up her spine. Her heart pounded in her chest. She'd learned at an early age to follow her instincts. Kneeling, she glanced around. Nothing. Except for the hidden creatures, they were alone.

Run.

Spanish moss dangling from the branches of the live oaks swirled, almost taunting her with agitation. Her breath rushed out. Plenty of lore had been passed around about the Bayou's grayish-green tinsel. Some believed the natural decoration of the Bayou had a life of its own, with its eerie atmosphere and use in Voodoo.

Her hands trembled. She almost pulled back from him, but forced herself to clasp his shoulder, gently shaking him. "It's me, Teva. I'm back."

Flee while you can.

Teva's breath caught as creatures plopped into the sleeping water of the nearby river. Nervously, she scanned the area.

Nothing.

She concentrated on waking him. Again and again, she attempted to rouse him. Finally, an inhuman sound of pain rumbled out of his chest.

On a gasp, she jerked her hands away. "Can...can you hear me?"

Escape.

The sky, visible through the canopy, clouded over, leaving behind early shadows elongating in the little glade. Her mouth went dry. Fear. She shoved it away. Why should she be afraid? She could be silly at times. The guy couldn't harm her. She didn't think he could stand. Besides, she'd get him to the hospital and never have to see him again.

She heaved until he lumbered to his hands and knees. She urged him up. "Come on, only a few feet and you can sit down."

The stranger's weight leaned heavily on her as she helped him to her jeep. Trembling, he slumped into the seat, eyes closed. Making sure his legs were out of the way, she shut the door.

With a final look around, she quickly circled the vehicle to climb in and revved it up. Once in gear, she winced as they were jolted.

They'd gone no more than a mile when a freak hailstorm opened up on them. The tires started to slide. She maneuvered back onto the path just as lightning struck the tree next to them and thunder roared its fury. Quickly, she rolled up her window. He covered his ears, groaning. Teva's heart thumped in her chest. Her palms coated with sweat as she gripped the steering wheel.

What was going on? She couldn't escape the storm. It seemed to be following them.

She changed direction away from the city and toward her home. It was too dangerous out. She couldn't see clearly from the nasty weather. She'd never make it to the city in this downpour. She'd call for an ambulance once she got home.

Their breath condensed on the windshield, clouding her view. Using frantic motions, she wiped it with her palm.

The stranger continued to groan and cover his ears.

"We'll be inside soon," she assured him.

The hail came down in softball-sized projectiles now. A freak storm. She shivered to her toes. Finally making it to her home, she pulled right into the garage, thankful when the door came down behind them.

The stranger's breathing had eased. "Hang on a sec. I'll be right back." Her feet raced across the concrete and then wood floor until she snatched up the phone.

No dial tone.

How could this be? She blew out a breath. Next, she tried her cell that she'd left on the battery charger.

No service.

It was always hit-and-miss living in a remote area, but what a crappy time to have let the battery run down. Bottom lip caught between her teeth, she gazed around.

Think. You've lived through a natural disaster. Pull it together and deal. It's now up to you to care for him.

Long strides carried her to her spare bedroom. The room was full of clutter since it doubled as her office. With jerky motions, she made her guest a place to rest.

Back at the jeep, the guy's skin was scalding to her touch. He had a raging fever and murmured incoherently.

"Shh...come on, I have to get you inside." She tugged on his arm. "Come on, guy, you've got to help me." She tried not to focus on the fact that she was touching a naked male or notice how his muscles rippled as he moved. She eased his leg around, and he swung his other one to the floor. Teeth clenched, he stood for her. She shimmied under his arm. "Okay, we have to go through the kitchen and down a hall. You can rest soon."

He grunted, then moved his legs one after another.

God, was he heavy.

She was breathing as harshly as he was by the time they reached the hallway. "Not far now. Come on."

He stumbled but managed to stay on his feet. Inside the room, he simply collapsed on the bed. He watched her with glazed eyes. Quickly, she worked his feet on the bed and covered him. Rushing to the medicine cabinet, she collected a pain reliever, to hopefully help ease his aches and pains and break his fever. She snatched up a water bottle from the kitchen, hurrying back to his side. "Are you allergic to anything?"

"No." His eyes never left hers. He seemed as wary of her as she felt about him. Thankfully, he took the medicine and drank the water without another word.

"The phone line is down. As soon as I can, I'll call for an ambulance to take you to the hospital."

His perfect mouth twisted. "Stop this game."

"Game?" She frowned. "Who's playing a game?"

His eyes dropped closed. "My masters, who else?" His mouth went slack in sleep.

His masters? Just how delusional was this guy? She prayed it was the fever and he wasn't actually insane. This was far riskier than bringing home a stray animal which she'd had a habit of doing.

Listening to the hail continue to come down on the roof, Teva set about making him a little more comfortable in his sleep.

Lash woke, his mouth stuck from dryness. His body ached from a recent battering. No denying he'd been beaten once again. Puzzlement clouded his mind. After a sleep he should feel refreshed, not sluggish. His kind had the ability to rejuvenate. All the better to heap more tortures on them.

Silence.

He heard nothing. There was no howling from the enraged. No screams of agony. No cries of despair. Did he dare open his eyes?

No.

He'd wait. The legion lords were up to something. All too quickly he'd learned never to trust a demon.

Stomach churning with nausea and fear, he willed them to attack him. To get it over with. How long had passed since he'd awakened? It seemed another eternity and still no retribution. He cracked open an eye to discover no leering face before him.

Nearby, the woman sat curled up asleep on a chair. He glanced around. He was in a room of some sort. The keepers used rooms for torture or imprisonment. The nausea grew. Something very wrong had happened.

No.

He was being tested. She'd spring up wild-eyed any moment and gouge his eyes out for daring to look her way. How many times had it happened in the past? Too many times to count.

So he lay there, hoping his breathing didn't disturb her. He dozed, only to awaken to the feel of a soft touch. Startled, he gazed at her through lowered lashes.

"Good, you're awake. I've been worried. Your fever broke hours ago. Are you hungry? Thirsty?" She smiled. His breath caught at her loveliness. Short red curls bounced around a heart-shaped face. Clear blue eyes held his gaze. "I'll be back in a minute. I'll get you some soup."

He listened to the scuff of her feet as she walked along the floor, hearing no click of claws.

Odd.

You could *always* hear the click of claws.

He kept his gaze lowered when she reentered the room. She sat on the side of the bed. "I don't know what's going on with the weather. It's been storming and raining for a day now." Brow furrowed, she sighed. "Still no phone service."

He stared at the bowl in her hand. Would she burn him? Make him eat poison that would tear his insides up?

"Here. Open up." She held a spoonful out to him. Her lips curved into a soft smile. "Hey, don't look like that. I make a good chicken broth."

There was no choice but to do as a keeper instructed. He

opened his mouth and swallowed what she offered. He moaned. Not from pain, but pleasure. The liquid was tasty. How long had it been since he'd eaten anything good? His stomach churned. What was she thinking? Was it a new form of torment? It could still kill him again. A million deaths weren't good enough for his kind.

He shivered, and she offered him another bite. "This will warm you up." His tongue lingered over the salty flavor before swallowing. She offered him bite after bite. He took his time eating. His eyelids were heavy when she dropped the spoon into the empty bowl.

"Do you want to use the bathroom?" Her face took on a red tinge.

He didn't want to visit any other rooms. *Ever.* This was the nicest room he'd ever been in. At least, from what he could remember. "Bathroom?" he asked, in case she expected it of him.

"I mean, do you need to go...um...pee...or..." Her hand fluttered. "You've slept a day away."

Unsure, he swallowed. What did she want from him? His kind was never given a thought or care. They were only ordered about or abused.

She shrugged. "Maybe later. Let me know if you need any help." Her hand fluttered once more. "If not, it's right across the hall..." She stood up. "I'm going to see if I can get anything on the radio about the weather. Get some more sleep."

The bathroom was to pee in. He never broke rules. Lash nodded, again listening for the click of claws. He closed his eyes when he heard none of the usual signs of the legion lords. His skull throbbed. It was too hard to think right now.

He dozed, coming to with a strong urge to relieve himself. His bladder was so full, it ached. He held his breath, listening.

Hearing nothing, he rose up and moved to the edge of the bed. Standing, he trembled. How long had it been since he'd been allowed to stand to his full height?

At the hallway, he looked both ways to check for the mistress. The door was closed across the hall. Turning the knob, he swung the door open.

Lash sucked in a breath. She stood there staring at him. Large, full breasts. He licked his lips as her nipples swelled, pebbled under his stare. His gaze slid lower along a rounded belly. Smooth, curved thighs. Red curls hid her sex. His cock engorged to stand straight out in front of him.

"Take her!" A voice urged him to claim the temptation.

He clenched his fists in refusal.

"You know you want a piece of her sweet pussy."

He glanced around the little room. He recognized that gravelly voice. It belonged to none other than the Prince of Netherworld.

"Oh my God! I know that door was locked." She snatched up a towel, wrapping it around her soft curves.

Through lowered lashes he watched her. The door had not been locked, but only a fool disagreed with a keeper. His nostrils flared. Her nipples were still hard underneath the towel. He could smell her arousal now.

His cock pulsed, and he ground his teeth fighting the hunger of both want and need.

"Spread her white thighs and fuck her! Fuck her hard!"

Lash's heart raced. Who tormented him now? Abdiel? Most likely.

"Take her," the Prince taunted.

A brutal appetite curled in his groin. He wanted to fuck her. Wanted it enough to suffer another lifetime in the eternal darkness.

"Push your cock into her slick pussy! Fuck her!"

He took a step forward.

Then another.

How enticing her pussy looked, with its red curls peeking out from just below the towel. How delicious she would be writhing under him, making his cock slick with her moisture. Urging him to come with the clenching of her inner walls. His cock was so rigid, his hips thrust forward in need. He growled with hunger.

The mistress gasped, protectively tightening her hold on her towel. Her pretty blue eyes were now wide with fear.

Fear.

He could taste it. His own as well as hers. Sweat beaded on his brow as a horrid realization sank in. A mistress among the legion lords wouldn't fear him. She would have no reason to.

"I'm sorry, mistress." Dazed, he backed away from her and then out of the room. What had she said when she'd come upon him? *My name is Teva Gibson.*

Now he understood the slowness with which he'd healed. The lords and their power...

Lust forgotten, Lash whimpered like a newborn babe. He closed his eyes as he backed into a doorframe.

Please, Lord...no... He knew it was hopeless. He'd been forgotten long ago by the All-Powerful and any part of Him. But Teva... Surely she hadn't been forsaken.

Lash grasped his head as his tormentors let loose their displeasure. Thunder cracked outside. The sky flashed with lightning outside the windows. His teeth rattled. His ears rang. His skull pounded. He dropped to his knees. He couldn't get his breathing to regulate. It rushed out of his lungs.

Soft hands grasped his shoulders. "Let's get you back to bed."

"No." He shrugged her off. "Don't touch me. Don't ever touch me."

A battering ram slammed his mind, and in temporary peace his world went black.

Chapter Two

"Welcome back," Teva greeted him as Lash opened his eyes. "I'm glad you didn't sleep too long this time." The mistress sat cross-legged on the floor beside him. "I was worried when you passed out."

He worked his tongue in his mouth to relieve its dryness. "I'm sorry I frightened you, mistress."

"Call me Teva, and I'm fine." She shrugged her shoulders. "I must have forgotten to lock the door. I only have a tub in my bathroom, so when I'm in a hurry I shower in the spare one."

She hadn't forgotten. One of the lords had manipulated it with magic. They were powerful beings. The sight of her nakedness rushed back to him. Such beauty should never be allowed near him, or any of his kind. He closed his eyes.

"Hey, big guy, you ready to get up off the floor?"

A soft pillow had been placed under his head and his body was covered as well. The floor wasn't uncomfortable. No, he'd known plenty of worse beds in Netherworld.

He pushed to his feet, since she encouraged him to. Once standing, she waved a hand. "The bathroom is free now."

He nodded and walked into the small room. With confusion he glanced around. Baths he remembered, and if you wanted to risk one in Netherworld, you had any of the five rivers that ran through the kingdom to use. Where did one piss in this world? In Netherworld there were no designated areas.

Lash turned around. "Mistress...I'm not... " He glanced down to the low white stool on the floor. That was his guess, but being wrong had always cost him severely.

She moved forward, her pretty face flushed. "Oh...um...maybe you hurt your head?" A frown marred her forehead. "Does your head hurt? You could have amnesia."

"No. My head no longer hurts." In truth, he felt better than he had in a long time. "I don't know of this amnesia."

"Oh, it's where you hurt your head and lose part of your memory. But don't worry, it'll all come back after some rest." She'd lowered her gaze, giving him the impression she wasn't convinced it'd come back.

He almost told her he didn't have amnesia, but then he stopped himself. He'd use this illness to his advantage to learn what he needed in this world.

"Well, let's see..." She waved to the tub behind him. "For bathing." She moved around before turning knobs to cause water to spray. "For showers." Once the water was off, she touched containers hanging inside the bath. "For your hair and for your body."

He nodded, already liking the shower feature.

"And over here we have a sink." Again, she turned knobs off and on. "For your hands and face. Oh, here, let me get you a spare toothbrush."

Intently, he watched as she opened little doors. She placed another container on the sink. "Toothpaste and brush."

He nodded.

"Towels are hanging right behind you. And lastly, the toilet..." Face flushed, she leaned over and pushed a metal handle. Water swirled around. "For your business."

"Thank you."

"You're very welcome. Why don't you clean up? And I'll make you something to eat?"

He nodded, but she'd already backed out of the room.

Quickly, he pissed and showered. After brushing his teeth, he made sure everything was in the exact places she'd had them stored.

Once back in his bed, he listened to his surroundings. He didn't hear the storm any longer, though that didn't mean the legion lords couldn't produce another if it suited them.

Soft footfalls earned his attention at the doorway. Teva entered the room, carrying a tray. "I brought you several things. More broth, Jell-O, and a popsicle." Her eyes sparkled. "All the things they'd give you in a hospital."

His stomach rumbled as he sat up. Teva set the tray on the bed and moved to the chair.

Fingers splayed, he picked up the bowl and drank the warm liquid in one long swallow.

"Oh my..." She laughed. "You do like that broth. I'll bake some chicken for you later today."

The brew had been warm and tasty. He licked his lips before looking at the remaining offerings. Neither of them looked appealing. Taking the stick in his hand, he quickly brought it to his mouth and bit down. Cold engulfed his senses.

"Oh, I should have reminded you. Popsicles are to be sucked."

The red popsicle was sweet, but he'd have rather had more broth.

Using his spoon, he scooped up most of what must be the wiggly Jell-O and stared down at the glob. It was a blob of some sort. Closing his eyes, he risked a taste. It too was sweet, but he liked it better than the popsicle.

"Do you remember your name?"

His head came up sharply. *His name?* She wanted to know his name. It had been so long since he'd given it a thought. "Nicodemus."

"Nicodemus." She smiled, her eyes lighting up.

The use of his name from her lips aroused him. He shifted in the hopes of hiding his rising desire.

"Quite a name. You're not from around here. Do you know your last name?"

She had a tempting mouth. He shook his head. His people didn't use last names. "I'm known as Lash."

"Lash. Puts me in mind of Guns N' Roses. You know, 'cause of Slash."

He didn't mean to remind her of guns. He hated the weapons. Too many times a lord had played a game with one. He hated to hear the click of an empty chamber pressed to his head—even worse, when the cartridge exploded in his brain. Too often a demon had killed him in such a way out of pleasure, only to revive him later for another round of torture.

"Not a big rock and roll fan, huh? It's my favorite genre of music."

Setting the tray aside, he swung his legs to the floor. "Do you have rocks you wish for me to move?"

"Move rocks?"

"Yes, mistress." He'd spent years in the mines. He didn't mind the labor compared to other backbreaking chores.

"Oh, no. I was talking about music..."

Music? Rocks did not make music. But when used by a legion lord, they could often kill a slave.

"Oh, never mind." She scooted to the edge of her chair. "How about I call you Nic? And how about you call me Teva?"

Nic. He'd never been called the name before and didn't think it was a good idea, yet he nodded to make her happy.

"Great." She smiled. "The storm seems to have cleared. I think we should take you to the hospital."

The hair on the back of his neck stood on end. *A hospital.* He knew of hospitals. The demons used them to house their mutations. Often slaves were experimented on for the lords' amusement.

Carefully, he shook his head.

"I'm concerned you may have loved ones looking for you. A hospital could have access to more help than I can provide." She wrung her hands.

"I have no loved ones. No one is looking for me." He closed his eyes. Thankfully, his parents and older brother had made it to the Afterworld. The legion lord took pleasure in telling him they'd gone on without him. Yes, they lived in Paradise and surely never gave his lost soul a thought. "I don't need a hospital."

Her full lower lip disappeared as she sucked it between her teeth. His balls tingled, and he lowered his gaze. Teva's mouth intrigued him in unfamiliar ways.

"Nic?"

Quickly, he looked up.

"I'm going to be honest. I'm torn. Half of me wants to take you to the hospital, but your eyes are so expressive. I know you don't want to go."

The steady beat of his heart sped up. Yes, he'd known he could hide little from the outside world. The demon lords liked knowing everyone's thoughts and had ensured the fact that their slaves' eyes remained mirrors to their souls.

"How about I take your picture? I have a friend who can check to see if you're missing anywhere."

With a nod, he gave his consent. As long as he could stay here, he'd agree with anything she wanted.

"Great. I'm going to get you some clothes while I'm out." A wide smile spread across her mouth. Pleasure stirred inside him. He'd pleased her. "Give me a second to collect a few things." Red curls bouncing, she snatched up the tray and left him alone.

The sensible thing would be to get the guy to the hospital. For the first time in her life, Teva was going to be reckless. Nic had no fever and no swelling. The bruises looked much better. Her instincts told her he was fine. The desire he inspired assured her he was very, very *fine*.

It was the man's response that kept her from pressuring him to go to the hospital. When he'd first entered the bathroom, she was still sure she'd locked it. She'd been startled, then sexually aroused.

Again, sensations fluttered low in her belly. Nic turned her on. Oh, who was she kidding? The guy would turn on anyone with eyesight.

Her excitement had stirred at the sight of him. Her body had thrilled with the prospect of what he could do to her. Thighs quivering, she sat on the edge of her bed for a moment.

Stop it!

"Are you nuts?"

He could have raped her. She shivered. Not a chance of it being rape.

Erotic. The experience had been erotic. Part of her had

wanted to be taken by the stranger. A very wanton part.

Teva's face, along with the rest of her body, heated.

Dark and dangerous, he'd looked like a god of eroticism standing in the doorway, with his cock at full attention. Her sex had grown moist. Ached. She'd longed to drop to the floor and beg him to take her.

But it'd been the fear that had slashed across his eyes that drove her to help him. Nic feared her. It'd been her that he'd reacted to. That unnerved her most of all.

Considering her reaction to Nic, she was half tempted to dig out her old family spell journal for a healing or, dare she think it, love potion... Too bad she'd promised her mother she'd never follow in her family's footsteps.

Pushing to her feet, she located a tape measure and her digital camera. Nic lay flat on his back when she joined him once more. "Okay, if you haven't changed your mind about going to the hospital..."

Carefully, she watched him. He didn't make a single wince as he sat up. "I'm sure."

She sighed. He had one of the roughest voices she'd ever heard. It put her in mind of a pro football coach that'd ruined his voice from yelling. "Then let me get your picture."

It took her a moment to get the camera ready. She didn't use it often. Turning the digital camera on, she focused and clicked a picture.

He blinked in reaction to the flash, and she took another. This one was strictly for her own pleasure. Once he was gone, she'd enjoy them.

While he didn't say a word, he stared curiously at the camera, and she sat beside him to show him the pictures. "They turned out nice."

Gently, he took the equipment from her hand to gaze at the images. "This is me? In the box?"

"Well, your likeness." She grinned, only to feel guilty. Perhaps he did need to see a doctor for his amnesia. Maybe in a day or two, if there was no change.

"I have no scars." He murmured so low, she barely caught it.

Tilting her head, she looked at him. Scars? The guy was pure sin to look at. A mouth-watering male. Perfect. Large. Broad. Muscular. "Do you remember something? Something about scars?"

He handed the camera back. "I don't know."

Since she didn't know if she should push him, she didn't.

Standing, she unrolled her tape. "I'm guessing you're an extra large." She frowned. "Maybe a double X." He looked like he'd fit right into any of the pro football teams she loved to watch. "Am I right?"

He simply stared.

She'd thought as much. "I'll need to measure your waist and inseam for a pair of jeans." She'd get him some clothes. Though the idea of keeping him around naked tempted her reckless side.

When his expression didn't change, she encouraged him with a wave of her hand. "Come on, I won't bite." She surveyed that yummy body. For him, maybe she'd make an exception and buy designer brands. Her tongue swirled around her bottom lip. "If I leave now, I can be back with some clothes for you by dark."

Nic stood.

It was her turn to stare. God, the guy was perfection and had no sense of modesty. His long, thick cock once again stood straight out at attention. Heat spread up from her loins. Her nipples pebbled as her pussy pooled moisture.

I swear, I'm not keeping him here to ogle him.

Never before had such arousal been awakened in her. Never had she experienced the sweet, exquisite sensations that Nic invoked. Just looking at him, her panties dampened.

Rushing around to the back of him, she sought to catch her breath. With her lower lip caught between her teeth and eyes closed, she wrapped the tape measure around his waist before checking the number.

Glancing down, she licked her lips.

What a delectable backside. Her fingers twitched with agitation, tempted to squeeze a butt cheek.

Do it. A feminine voice poured in her mind.

Teva gasped at its oddly familiar tone.

Do it. Better yet, lick that round, delectable ass.

Heart beating a mad pace and her clit pulsing to match, she took his inseam measurement. "I need to measure your foot." She'd try to get a shoe to fit him this way.

He presented a foot for her and she measured it from heel to big toe.

Though she was tempted to linger, she forced herself to stand. "Think I've got everything I need." Picking up her camera, she headed for the door. "I'm going to throw some dinner in the oven. Why don't you rest while I'm gone?"

Silently, he nodded.

☙

Lash's guts knotted. It grew dark, and Teva hadn't returned

yet. He rolled over, clutching the pillow. No one was safe in the dark. It'd been the first lesson he'd learned in Netherworld. He willed sleep to claim him, but it wasn't working. He wanted Teva to return.

The hair along his arms stood on end, along with those on his head. He smelled the creature before it appeared.

Not daring to open his eyes, he lay still.

A shudder wracked his frame as the cover was pulled away from his body.

He swallowed.

"Enjoying your vacation from our kingdom?" Asmodeus snarled, while he climbed up onto the bed to cover Lash's body with his own.

Bile rose up his throat at the demon lord's grotesque body pressed against his all-too-sensitive one. Asmodeus, lord of lust, pressed his engorged cock along Lash's ass.

Lash balled his fists into the pillow.

"How tempted I am to ravish that unscarred body of yours. The Prince put you together as good as new, didn't he?"

Fighting back the gag reflex from the lord's vile breath, he forced a nod.

Viciously, his head was yanked back by his hair. "Answer me."

"Yes, master." He gritted his teeth. His neck could be broken and repaired until the legion lord grew tired of the torture.

"That's better." A rough tongue ran up his throat, making him gag. "I remember when you were tossed into Netherworld," Asmodeus continued on a purr. "You're as beautiful today as you were then. Yes, the Prince chose well. The pretty cunt won't be able to resist your dark masculinity."

Lash shuddered at the pumping of the demon's cock along his ass.

"We're going to leave you alone for a spell so you can get acquainted with Teva Gibson, but when we return, be prepared to ruin the bitch." The legion lord's breath turned ragged as its cock rubbed along his body.

Lash held his breath at what would happen next. The evil fiend took perverse pleasure in sexual torture. In a few heartbeats, come squirted across his back. He swallowed down the nausea.

Asmodeus groaned, pushing up from the bed. "There's a spot in Netherworld for Teva's pretty cunt already reserved. And when you return home, you can bet I won't just be taking a dry hump."

Then the demon's stink was gone, and Lash let out a breath.

On shaky legs, he stumbled into the bathroom to shower once more. Quickly, he cleaned the sticky residue from his body and turned the water hotter. He hunched down on the shower floor, making himself smaller.

His skin still crawled. He wanted to be clean. There wasn't a chance of that ever happening.

He couldn't save himself. Netherworld was his home and would be for all eternity. He'd spend forever making up for his sins, for his hatred of his enemy, the powerful Olympians. His eternity was payment for his wrathful vengeance against them. But maybe he could save Teva. She'd been kind.

Besides his family, hers was the only kindness he ever remembered. She had a pure soul. He didn't want to help the Netherworld lords claim someone so undeserving.

Chapter Three

Finally arriving back home, she climbed from the jeep and grabbed the bags. Kicking the door closed, she trudged up to the front door. Not once in her life had she anticipated arriving home as much as she did now.

Nic. Her thoughts had barely left him while she'd taken care of business. Now all she wanted to do was make sure he was still there.

With a hip, she pushed the door open. After setting the bags down, she put some broccoli and carrots on to steam. If he'd split, she'd still have to eat. Not that a gorgeous *naked* guy could have gotten far without attracting attention...

With the bags containing his clothes in her hands, she headed to the guestroom. At his bedroom door, her heart lodged in her throat.

Please let him still be here.

A smile played across her lips at the sight of him. The guy was so gorgeous. Slowly, he rolled his head, and she looked into his black eyes.

"Hey."

"Hey." He pushed to a sitting position. The blanket fell dangerously low around his hips.

"Sorry I was gone so long." She'd spent too long at old man Jackson's place. The old deputy had pulled some strings. Using a fax machine, they'd learned Nic's picture didn't have a match in either the state or federal databases. There were no outstanding warrants for his arrest. After that, she'd relaxed.

Nic was just a guy who needed her help.

Playing the part of a Good Samaritan had always appealed to her. More so now than ever.

"I got you some clothes." She placed the shopping bags on the bed. Heat spread up her neck. "I wasn't sure if you were a boxer or briefs man...so I got you boxer briefs." Buying his clothes had been the most amazing experience. She'd not only gotten hot thinking of him in them, but she'd enjoyed the chore.

"Boxer briefs?" He pulled the plastic bags to his side.

"You know, underclothes."

His puzzled look intrigued her. She hadn't expected him to have forgotten about underwear...unless maybe he hadn't bothered with it before...

Commando.

Heat pooled in her lower region. "Um...if you're more comfortable..." She waved a hand awkwardly. "I can take them back." She hadn't experienced giddiness like this since she'd been in college and wound up in a closet with a linebacker.

"I'll wear whatever you think best." He didn't look inside the bags.

"You'll find jeans, t-shirts, socks, and a pair of pajama pants in there, along with a pair of boots." Arousal burned hot between her legs. What had she been thinking? "Um, you don't have to bother with the pajama pants...I want you to be comfortable." If the guy didn't wear underwear, he surely wouldn't wear pants to bed.

"Thank you."

Teva rubbed her suddenly sweaty palms on her jeans. "Great. Why don't you get dressed, and if you feel like getting up we can eat in the kitchen."

"Kitchen?" A slight tremor ran through his big body.

"It's down the hall. Follow your nose." With an encouraging smile, she reluctantly left him to dress.

Antsy and killing time, she set the table. Minutes later, Nic showed up in the kitchen doorway. Suddenly breathless, she moved to his side.

The guy looked as good in clothes as he did out of them. They fit him just right. She was glad she'd gone with the XXL t-shirts. She could image him in nice clothes too, instead of the bargain clothes she'd picked up. Hiding a smile, she removed the tags on his shirt and jeans.

Silently, he watched her movements with unblinking eyes.

"You hungry and ready for something more than Jell-O?"

He nodded.

She motioned to the table and moved to the stove. "Have a seat. I'll grab the food."

A chair scraped the floor. Glancing over her shoulder, she watched him settle onto a seat. His movements were so careful, so precise. "You want some music on?"

"Music?"

"Um...whatever genre you want." She shrugged. "You know, some background noise."

Another visible shudder racked his body. This time, she frowned and pulled the chicken from the oven.

"No. The quiet is peaceful."

She offered him another smile. "It is. You can't beat peace."

She loaded his plate up and set it on the table. "You want water or milk to drink? I have OJ, too."

"Water."

"Great." She filled a glass and put it alongside his plate.

He drained the glass before she had time to collect her meal.

Retrieving the cold water jug from the fridge, she placed it within easy reach of Nic. "Have all you want. There's plenty."

"Thank you." He drained another glass.

Once in her chair, she sensed his gaze following her movements. Peeking through her lashes, she noted he followed her lead with the utensils. What a puzzle he was. She ached to care for him as she had the homeless pets of her childhood. The thought somehow didn't feel right. Considering his size, no one could deny he should be able to care for himself.

Yet despite his predatory posture and dominating size, there was something vulnerable about him.

They ate in silence, until she offered him more chicken, which he accepted with another "Thanks". She'd never met a guy so polite before. His actions only increased her curiosity.

"Tomorrow I have a neighbor stopping by to examine you. She's a licensed nurse practitioner."

He looked up from his plate.

"I hope you don't mind, but since you don't want to go to the hospital, I think someone should check you out."

His bottomless black eyes simply stared.

"You haven't changed your mind about the hospital, have you?"

"No, no hospital."

"Great. You'll like Jenna."

He nodded.

"You want to have dessert on the porch?"

ೂ

The next morning, Lash sat still with his back to a tree. His breath caught as the landscape unfolded and the sun slowly rose across the horizon. Dark surrendering to purple and red, then finally gold. Amazing. It was a sight he'd never expected to see again. Netherworld had only gray, and a thick smog that often clogged your throat and burned your eyes.

He sighed.

The night had been just as unexpected. He'd slept in peace for the first time since he couldn't remember when.

No screams.

No torture.

No moans of utter despair.

He wasn't fooling himself by allowing the magic of the moment to sway him. It wouldn't last, and in no time he'd be back in the pits of Netherworld. Where he belonged. This was the worst torture, to see this beauty and all he was experiencing, to know it was just going to be ripped away from him when the lords decided. He would do what he could to keep them from taking this from Teva.

Footfalls approached. "Hey you, I've been calling your name."

He glanced up. He hadn't heard Teva. She must have been calling for Nic. He'd discovered last night, sometimes he didn't notice when she said Nic. He'd spent eons answering to Lash.

"Breakfast is served." She passed him a plate.

His stomach rumbled at the new scents. Balancing the

plate in one hand, he used his other to grasp the fork and cut into the flat bread. Bringing a chunk to his mouth, he moaned at the first bite.

"French toast is my favorite."

He nodded. He'd never had the treat, but it was now his favorite as well.

She allowed him to eat in silence. When he'd finished, he licked his plate clean, savoring every drop of the sticky syrup.

Passing the empty plate to her, he ignored her curious look and drank the water.

Cold water was his all-time favorite drink. After the heat he'd experienced, the water was refreshingly cold. Though, Netherworld could be extremely cold, too. Cold enough to take your life.

"You want some more?" A smile played on her lips. He appreciated the fact a smile came easily to her. He liked her good nature.

"Yes." What would she taste like covered in syrup... He closed his eyes, halting the image.

"Okay. Let's go inside."

Following her indoors, he was tempted by the seductive sway of her hips. In the kitchen, she worked at the stove while he sat at the table.

Teva had a nice home. It was something he could easily get used to.

"Eat up." She placed two more slices of bread on his plate. "Jenna will be here soon."

Without being told twice, he finished his meal. Teva jumped at the sound of a knock.

Quickly, she moved away from him to allow her friend to enter. The black woman was as round as she was tall, with a dazzling smile.

He nodded when Teva introduced him.

Jenna placed a bag she carried on an empty chair. "Honestly, I'd keep him all to myself, too." She elbowed Teva, whose face flushed. "I hear you've taken a knock to your noggin."

Lash stared, unsure of what a noggin might be.

Teva settled into the chair beside him. "We're not sure what happened to him, but my guess is he hit his head."

He frowned. Noggin meant head. He'd have to remember that.

"Why don't you take your shirt off, and I'll get a look at you?" The black woman winked at Teva.

Teva shook her head. "Jenna..."

Lash removed his shirt.

"He sure looks fit to me." Jenna passed Teva another wink.

Instantly, Teva's flushed face matched her red curls. He was tempted to smile. He enjoyed seeing her flustered.

He sat still and did as he was instructed as the woman examined him. He didn't care for the light shone directly into his eyes, but he didn't say so.

As the woman moved around to his back, she gasped.

He stiffened as dread slowly crawled up his spine. Did his scars show on his back? Did she see how truly grotesque he'd become?

"What?" Teva whispered.

Cautiously, Jenna moved around him, tossing her things into her bag. "He has the mark of the devil." Her hands trembled.

He closed his eyes. Of course, he'd been marked. All the

condemned bore a symbol of the Prince's everlasting ownership.

"Oh, Jenna, don't be silly."

At Teva's first step, he stood, slipping his shirt over his head, yanking it down with shaking hands.

Teva would hate him soon.

Worse.

She'd fear him.

"Girl..." Jenna lumbered away. "If there's one thing I don't joke about, it's the devil." She sprinkled some sort of dust on the floor.

A frown creased his brow. He was unsure of the reasoning behind dirtying Teva's floor.

"So he's got a birthmark." Teva waved a hand. "No big deal."

"This is nothing to fool around with." Jenna closed her bag and picked it up. "You go to my cousin's Voodoo shop, Ally Cease in the French Quarter. If anyone can help you, she can." Jenna backed away, reaching for the front door behind her. The woman now looked at him as if he were Cerberus, the ravenous three-headed dog of Netherworld.

Not trusting the legion lords, he reached up and touched his head. *Only one.* "I mean neither of you any harm."

Jenna shook her head, jerking the door open. "Girl, don't let his sinful good looks or charming tongue fool you." She kissed some type of leather pouch around her neck. "He's pure evil and wears a mark to prove it."

"I don't lie." None of the lost souls dared. They already paid for their sins. Lying wouldn't help them avoid any punishment, and none risked adding to the infractions they were already being punished for. At least, not many pushed for more punishment. And never him.

Teva followed Jenna out the door. He moved forward to listen to the women.

"Jenna, don't be this way. Nic's been through enough."

Wide-eyed, the black woman dashed off the porch as fast as possible. "You have no clue."

He followed in hopes of staying in hearing range.

"Look, it's probably some birthmark that looks like…oh, what is that sign? Six-six-six." Teva followed, her voice frantic.

"I'm telling you, that's not the sign that man is wearing." Jenna approached an object like Teva had transported him in yesterday. She pulled the door open. "He's fine, other than being cursed." She climbed into the vehicle and closed the door.

Teva groaned and threw up her hands.

"Remember my cousin." Then Jenna was moving away.

Teva shook her head. Forcing a fake smile, she approached him. "Don't pay her any mind. Her family is deeply superstitious."

He gazed at her lovely face, memorizing every detail. "Maybe you should see what her cousin has to say."

The sky suddenly cracked with lightning. His head pounded as he was engulfed by the vile scents of Netherworld.

☙

Home. He'd been brought home. The light was gone now. Only gloom surrounded him. The air had a heavy, offensive smell. It hung with an acrid tinge of decay mixed into a sickly-sweet perfume to cover the stink of death. It turned Lash's stomach.

He fought down the overwhelming urge to vomit.

Netherworld.

Where he belonged.

He whimpered like a newly delivered lost soul. At least there would be no surprises for him. No, this time he was prepared for his existence. No regrets this time either. He'd done right by Teva. Maybe his words would act as a warning.

Yes, thankfully, this time he'd be equipped to deal with what came his way.

A shiver raced along his nerve endings. There would be no reprieve. No deferment like before. The continual healing effect allowed him, along with the others, to be tortured for eternity, perpetually recovering, so that they all might be tormented again and again. Yes, it was his due as a lost soul.

Anamalech, the demon of bad news, leered in his face. "Guess what?"

Not caring for the games often played by the legion lords, Lash bowed his head.

A scream split the eerie quiet of Netherworld. He swallowed down the rising fear. Nothing that happened in this world could be prevented.

A sniveling black woman was dragged forward and dropped at his feet. The woman was perfect in face and form. Just like all newly arrived lost souls. Reborn in perfection only to have the demons strip it away with layer upon layer of scars.

Black eyes met his gaze.

Those eyes.

That mouth...

A low moan vibrated within his chest. *Dear Lord, no...*

Too late, he realized the demon had been inside his mind. Anamalech punched him in the side of his head, sending him sprawling beside Jenna Holliard. "Slave, you know there is only one *Lord* in our world."

"Yes, master." Lash grabbed his head to ease the ringing in his ears. He hated the legion lords' ability to listen to his thoughts.

Jenna clutched at him, babbling, "My car...my car..." Huge tears swam in her eyes. "My car...my car..."

The demon lord yanked him up by the hair. "Don't ever try to interfere with us again." He shook Lash like a rag doll and tossed him across the chamber. Bones cracked on impact against the stone wall.

Lash stumbled to his feet. Already, the bones were mending so they could be broken again.

"No. No. No," Jenna screamed with a quiver of madness as she was pulled to her feet. "This isn't real." She glared at him with accusing eyes. "You're playing a trick in my mind. I curse you!"

He looked on her with pity. His kind couldn't be cursed, for they were already the damned.

Byleth, one of the ruling dukes of Netherworld, stalked into the room. He waved a clawed hand. "Toss the bitch into the Acheron River."

A tremor raced along his bones. All too soon, she'd become accustomed to the invisible biting insects that stung. In no time, her body would be full of burrowing worms and parasites, leaving her nothing but a quivering mass of weeping flesh.

It was hard to say if that torture would be any worse than any other one the lords gleefully assigned in the world of darkness.

When Byleth's head turned his way, Lash kept his gaze lowered. The lord had a nasty temper and was easily provoked. The demon duke walked Lash's way until he stood in front of him. The powerful and deadly Dyleth lifted his chin, forcing Lash to meet his hate-filled gaze. "You'll try our patience no more, will you, slave?"

Lash swallowed. None of them could force him to harm Teva. None of them. He'd already lived through many tortures of Netherworld and feared none of them. So for the first time in eons he lied. He nodded. "No, master." He'd take more time with the woman before being returned to their torture, if they'd permit it.

CB

Instantly, the heat of the sun warmed him. He inhaled sharply, enjoying the peace of Earth once more.

Teva waved a hand in front of his face. "Hey, welcome back." A frown pursed her mouth. "You seemed to blank out there for a minute."

Had he only been gone a minute?

One had no sense of running time when it came to eternity.

In the distance, he caught sight of wafting smoke. Instinct told him its source. Jenna Holliard had left this place and would forever exist in Netherworld, like him.

Sadness and bitterness clogged his chest. He wanted no part of what was to come, or what had transpired. He had no wish to have Teva think ill of him.

He had learned that everyone, even the angels, had paths to follow, choices to make. Apparently, Jenna's future hadn't included the Afterworld of Paradise. The demons couldn't have claimed her otherwise.

With a sigh, he glanced down at the still-frowning Teva. "I'm thirsty."

"Let's go get you a glass of water." A gentle smile spread across her full lips as she clasped his arm. "And hey, promise me, don't worry about Jenna."

He nodded, his body warming to her touch. Worrying over the damned was a waste of energy.

Chapter Four

Teva wiped down the sink once she'd put the last dish away. She wasn't much calmer now than she'd been when Jenna had left.

What drama. She hadn't been expecting Jenna's behavior. The accusation. The scene had been far worse than anything she'd witnessed in her past. And teen girls and young women could get downright nasty... She pushed rising memories of high school and college from her mind.

Jenna hadn't been being mean. The woman had believed Nic was evil.

She glanced outside at Nic. He sat still under the same tree he'd been relaxing beneath earlier. An empty glass rested beside his hip.

Evil?

She had been worried upon first taking him in. Attraction had quickly replaced the worry. There was the chance Jenna was right and his looks and her growing attraction towards him had influenced her judgment. After all, in the past—a time or two—poor judgments had cost her when it came to a hunky guy.

No. A sixth sense told her he was anything but evil. When he'd said he meant her and Jenna no harm, she'd believed his oath.

Ogling him, she finished cleaning up from breakfast. As soon as the chore was complete, she joined him outside. "Hey."

Nic let an arm hang over his raised bent knee. The depths of his dark gaze met hers. His eyes. Never before had she encountered such openness in a gaze. She'd have thought with their black color, feelings, emotions would be better hidden. Not so.

Jenna's visit had spooked him.

She settled down near him. "Sorry about Jenna..."

"Don't be." He didn't blink. "She meant no harm."

"Well, she could've been a little less..." With a sigh, she crossed her legs Indian-style. "Direct."

In truth, Teva hadn't really noticed Nic's birthmark before. She'd been too concerned for his well-being...and well, he had been naked. Now, if his birthmark had been closer to his cock, she might have paid it more attention.

"Jenna's family is very religious." She supposed there wasn't a lot of difference between her pagan Celtic ancestry and Jenna's beliefs. Both groups were rooted in magic. With the right spell, both could pull from nature, as well as good or evil.

"Sometimes, what seems important to one will make no difference to another." Nic finally looked away.

"I'm not concerned about your birthmark." If only Jenna hadn't freaked over it, because right now Teva couldn't get it out of her mind.

"It's...not a birthmark." His voice was so low, she barely heard him.

It was her turn to stare in silence. Without being asked, he pulled his shirt over his head and turned his back so she could see his shoulder.

No. Not a birthmark. Or a tattoo. Some tattoos were

beautiful, even sexy. This was anything but.

How could she have ignored the marking? Though she'd been more concerned about injuries, she should have at least noted the design.

She gazed at his sculptured back, clearly defined with muscle. Perfect, all except the brand. She was pretty sure a brand had been burned into his skin, though she'd never seen one so intricate before.

The marking was as big as her hand or bigger. In the center, a pentagram held...

She looked closer.

An eye. The center of the pentagram was an eerie eye. What could be a lightning bolt shot outward from the right top of the pentagram. The other two buried symbols...she wasn't sure what they might be.

Compulsively, she reached out, but Nic scooted away. "No, don't." He pulled his t-shirt back on to hide the imperfection.

What exactly had Jenna said about the mark? Odd, but she couldn't recall the woman's words. Could barely recall Jenna's cousin's name. Ally Cease. There wouldn't be a need to contact the woman, yet the information couldn't hurt.

"Thank you for showing me."

He shrugged a shoulder. Glass in hand, he stood up to tower above her. "I'd like some more water."

"Oh, sure, you bet." She climbed to her feet. "I need to get some work done. Would you like to come along?"

He nodded.

"Great."

03

Lash's shoulder impacted with the doorframe as Teva's vehicle bounded along the rough road. She'd been talking since they'd left her home. He'd been grateful she hadn't pressed for information about his brand. Unsure if any of the legion lords watched his every move, he'd dared not risk more than show her the mark. A part of him had wished once she'd seen the proof of his damnation, she'd push him from her home.

Instead, she'd tried to touch the vile emblem.

"Nic?"

He glanced over.

"You okay? You want me to take you back home?"

Home. If she knew of his home, she'd run screaming from him. He should tell her…get it over with. But he couldn't. Not yet. More than a taste of freedom kept him quiet. Teva's every response intrigued him.

Releasing a breath, he rolled his head to look her way instead of at the passing land. "Tell me more of this work you do."

She smiled, only to look at the road they traveled over. "I bored you to sleep with my career."

"I wasn't sleeping."

She reached over to give his hand a squeeze. "I was teasing. Okay, here goes. Again…" She offered him another smile. "I run a land preserve that's been in my family for generations."

Ah…he knew what family meant.

"I have fifteen cabins I rent out to fishermen and scientists."

He'd fished in his old life. His brother had had a knack for catching the swimming creatures. Scientists, he didn't care for. They ruled in many of Netherworld's hospitals. And, while laws had kept many of them controlled on Earth, nothing held back their imaginations in the hospitals overlooked by demon lords.

Many of his kind believed once condemned to a hospital, there was no way of escape. Though he supposed —all in all— the tortures performed inside the hospitals could be no worse than any other punishments handed out to the lost souls.

"I get a lot of ecologists, plant and marine biologists, and naturalists out here."

Since he had nothing to add, he remained silent.

"Land conservation is so very important." She glanced his way. "Hey, last summer I had a crew from Animal Planet out here." She laughed. "Not impressed with talk of television? You are so not typical."

A grin tugged at his lips, but he bit it back. He'd never had a reason to smile before. Teva's happiness alone stirred an emotion he didn't dare explore.

"Anyway, there are some nice walking trails out here. And I've made arrangements with a couple of local guides for those who want a tour of the Bayou."

He nodded in encouragement. Her face was still animated, making it clear she enjoyed this talk of her land.

"So, now that you know what I do, can you remember what you do?"

I am a slave. A lost soul condemned to Netherworld.

"I...I was once a soldier." Though his race had been a gentle people for the most part, he had died in battle. If only his hate hadn't gotten the most of him. If only he hadn't wished to see the destruction of the Olympians and acted on the bloodlust. If only he hadn't followed his king's command. So many regrets that meant nothing.

"Oh, the military then? Do you recall which branch?"

Again, he'd said too much. So he shook his head and closed his eyes.

"Well, don't worry. Maybe I can find out for you? It might jog some memories."

"If you think it's best." He'd never discourage her from learning the truth about what he was, though he couldn't outright admit the truth to her.

"Great. I'll call Jackson soon and see what he thinks." She leaned over and rummaged through a box between the seats. She held up a thin round thing with a small hole in the center. "Do you mind some AC/DC?"

Forever had passed since anyone had asked him if he cared one way or another for something. He shook his head.

She pushed the thin disc into a slot, and a loud noise blared from the vehicle. And though he wasn't sure what the people from the vehicle yelled about, he preferred the sounds to the screams that dominated Netherworld.

Teva's fingertips tapped to the beat of the noise.

Down the road, a frown marred his forehead. Was Teva singing something about "Highway to Hell"?

When Teva stepped from the parked jeep, so did Lash.

"I've got three cabins I need to clean, and I've got a fallen tree blocking a trail." She shoved her hands into the back pockets of her jeans. Her breasts stood at attention. "Which should we tackle today?"

"I'm as capable at cleaning as I am at chopping, so you decide."

She groaned with a sparkle in her eyes. "So you're one of those that make another decide?"

Unsure what she meant, he looked away.

"Well, it's a nice day, so let's check the trail out. And I didn't bring you with me to work. You need your rest."

Sit while she worked? Hadn't she noticed his size? He could pull his weight and more. The legion lords had often compared him to ten souls. If she worked, he'd help her.

"Let me grab a few things from the jeep, and then we'll get some tools."

He waited while she went around to the back of the jeep. Holding some cloth shaped as hands, she climbed back inside to retrieve her keys. Using her hip, she pushed the door closed. "All set here."

The two walked to a small building and Teva used a key to unlock it. She opened the two doors wide and walked inside. Puzzled, he watched as she climbed onto a small four-wheeled machine with some sort of cart behind in it. The little vehicle roared past him, making a monstrous racket as it towed the cart.

What had happened to horses in this world? They had been such strong, magnificent animals.

He shook his head as Teva climbed off the now-rumbling machine. After collecting an ax from inside, she shut and locked the doors. "Okay, I think we're set. We can ride double."

He eyed the little machine as she climbed on. She wanted him to voluntarily climb onto it with her? It was too small for him, let alone the two of them. "I prefer a horse."

Her blue eyes widened. "You can ride a horse?"

"Yes." Well, he used to be able to ride a horse. He and his brother had spent long hours racing each other.

"That's great. There's a stable not far from here. Maybe it'll bring back some more memories." She settled onto the seat. "I'll run this baby slow, not that it's fast. I picked it up used."

He nodded and fell in step with her as she rode along. He wasn't worried. Speed had never been a problem of his. A legion lord told you to run, you ran as if the hounds of hell were after you. And for the most part, the hounds *were* chasing you. The loser of a race suffered an agonizing death.

"I'm sure the noise will be enough advance warning for any snakes, but be on the lookout anyway." Teva waved her hand in front of them as they started down a path. "Louisiana has several species of rattlers, copperheads, coral snakes, and the famous water moccasin."

"I don't fear serpents."

"They don't bother me much either, but it's always good to be cautious."

Pits of snakes were a favorite torture of the demons. A lord would push a lost soul into an opening, leave them there suffering bites and suffocation for months or years before they'd be pulled free for a new form of torment. Those afraid of serpents had a far worse time with the punishment.

With the drone of the four-wheeler, the two went along. Sometimes Teva would get a little ahead of him, only to drop back, allowing him to keep pace.

Repeatedly, his gaze drifted to the bounce of her breasts as the machine she rode went along the trail. Hs cock stayed swelled, enticed by the curve of her ass cradled on the seat.

At the fallen tree, Teva maneuvered the cart around so the little machine faced the way they'd walked. She backed the cart up as close as she could to the tree.

Lash picked the ax up from where she'd laid it on the flat of the cart. While the tree was about as thick as his thigh, it wouldn't be much of a chore. He'd once spent a decade in the metal forest of Netherworld.

He shuddered. Never would he forget how his spine would

jar and his tooth would rattle with each contact of his ax against a metal tree.

Yes, cutting an Earth tree into firewood would be no task at all.

"Hey, I'm doing the work." Teva pulled the cloth-like hands over her fingertips.

"No, mistress, I'll do the work while you relax." He pointed to the cart. "As payment for the clothes you've provided me."

"Well...I guess that seems fair, but please don't tire yourself. There's no hurry to get this done." She waved the cloth hands his way. "You want to see if these gloves fit?"

"No."

She sat on the edge of the cart.

The first strike of the ax barely registered in his shoulders. Strike after strike, he split the tree into blocks.

"You've obviously done this before."

"Yes."

"You remember it clearly, then?"

He hesitated with the next blow. He didn't want to lie, but he didn't want to tell her of his punishment in Netherworld's forest. "I just know I've done this before."

"Sure look like it when you tackle the chore. Thank you."

"You're welcome."

She sighed. "I love it out here."

"It's nice." He rolled a chunk out of the way and braced his foot for another swing of the ax.

After he'd cut a few chunks, Teva made her way over to start hauling the wood to the cart. He stopped chopping to help.

"If you're sure you're okay, I'm going to run back to the jeep..."

"Go ahead." He straightened to look her way.

"I forgot our water." She smiled. "I'm normally not absent-minded."

A smile attempted to pull his mouth up. He fought it as she unhooked the cart and climbed onto the little machine. He returned the wave she gave him.

Listening to the hum of her moving down the trail, he thought of nothing as he continued to hack the tree. Work was second nature to him, and welcome.

Lash was placing the last of what he'd already cut onto the cart when she pulled back up.

Her red curls glistened in the sun as she hopped off. "Hey, you thirsty?"

"Always."

She passed him a water container from a box.

His hand clutched the bottle. It was cool to the touch, which intrigued him. Yet it didn't distract him from the bead of sweat that slowly rolled down between Teva's lush breasts. The familiar lust stirred. His cock swelled, filling out his pants.

She reached over and removed the cap for him. After an initial sip, he guzzled down the cool drink. He handed the empty container back before wiping his forehead. He wanted to ask for another. In Netherworld, no one escaped the punishment of thirst. Never would he get enough water.

He got back to work, only to freeze when dread slowly crawled up his spine. He straightened to his full height.

"What is it?" Teva looked around.

Lash caught sight of the darken from the corner of his eye. The legion lords had sent a half-demon to spy on him. He'd hoped to be left alone for a while, but he should have known better.

A darken, a rotting lost soul, stared at him a long moment before disappearing.

"What's wrong?" Teva touched his arm. "I don't see anything."

No. She wouldn't be able to see a darken. He was thankful for that blessing. Darkens were at times more frightening than the demons that ruled Netherworld. The darkens would do anything to please the masters. All too easily, a lost soul could turn darken and in no time become a demon. As far as he knew, once a soul started to darken, there was no turning back.

"Hey, let's call it a day here. It'll be lunchtime soon." She took the ax and laid it on the cart along with the water box.

"Teva..." After seeing the darken he knew the lords had no intention of giving him time.

Her eyes questioned him.

He swallowed, knowing what he had to risk. "I want you to go see Ally Cease."

A lightning bolt hit him out of nowhere. Teva screamed as the electricity held him captive. Red dots flashed on the backs of his eyes as his body convulsed. He hit the ground hard and tried to swallow.

"Nic! Oh my God..." Frantic hands shook him. "Nic, don't die!"

It had been a long time since he'd experienced the violence of electricity. His nerve endings still sizzled. "I'm already dead." *I can't die. At least, not for long.*

"Nic!"

Chapter Five

Lash hung by his hands from poles set upon a high platform. His legs dangled limp with no support. The muscles across his shoulders and arms quaked. The whip ends applied hooks to the skin of his back, ass, and legs. The punisher used vicious force behind the swings. There was no escape for him now.

He'd been brought home to Netherworld once more. He'd been expecting it, had taken the risk to try to warn Teva.

Focusing on the panderers and seducers who crawled past him on their bellies, he worked to tune out the hot pain of his flesh being torn away. In life, the whimpering sinners had manipulated others to do their bidding. Now ugly demons forced the lost souls along with whips, much like the one being used on him. Sometimes the lords punished groups of sinners as a whole. And often times a demon liked to see the condemned crawl on their bellies.

He'd grown accustomed to ignoring the others' suffering.

The pain, he could cope with.

Teva's cries in his mind, he couldn't.

A shudder ran along his spine. He could almost feel her shaking him in an attempt to wake him.

Gremory, a breathtakingly beautiful female demon, appeared from out of nowhere. She kicked at the passing lost souls. The condemned crawled faster in hopes of escaping her sharp claws.

She waved her hand, and a large viewing screen appeared. In his lifetimes, he'd seen many a viewing screen, but he'd never known what it represented until now. Obviously he'd not been the first to have qualms about harming a human.

On the screen, Teva knelt on the ground, cradling his lifeless body. Tears flowed from her caring eyes.

"Turn it off." Lash finally spoke his first words since his return home. "Turn it off." He couldn't bear to watch Teva in her panicked state.

Gremory flipped her long red curls over her naked shoulder. "Slave, know who you speak to!" Her mouth twisted, revealing sharp canines. "Beat him harder."

The hooked whip ends cut into him in quick flashes of white-hot pain. There was no denying muscle was being torn away as his blood flowed down in rivulets.

He would suffer another death soon.

Gremory was momentarily distracted by a lost soul crawling by. She prowled over to a blond man and yanked him over to the platform from where he bled dark rivers of red. "What's your sin, slave?" Gremory pulled the man's head back by his hair.

How many times had he been in the same position as the now-moaning slave?

Too many. He took anything, so not to focus on the pain or Teva.

He stared into the man's black eyes, offering him what solace he was permitted.

"Seduction, mistress."

Gremory licked her lips. "Did you impregnate an innocent?"

The slave closed his eyes.

"Oh, what fun." She pulled the man closer. "Kneel between my thighs as I continue to enjoy the show." Their mistress shoved the man's face into her pussy. The slave slurped in his eagerness to please Gremory.

She moaned, grinding her pussy against the slave's mouth.

A hook caught the base of Lash's skull. The pain ignited, offering him only a second before he closed his eyes as another of his lives turned to dust.

Instantly, Lash woke once again, whole. He shook his head to clear it. Gremory now sat astride the lost soul's face, more than likely smothering the slave in her ecstasy.

The beating started up once more, tearing at his back.

On the screen, Teva held him while her frantic gaze drifted around the clearing they'd been working in.

A shudder racked his body. The punishment, he didn't mind. The deaths, he didn't mind. It was the never forgetting a moment of it all that drove him almost mad at times.

The legion lords would still expect him to comply with their wishes.

On screen, Teva held him captive. No matter what was done to him, he wouldn't harm her. He couldn't.

He looked back at the mistress. How could he escape their wishes while keeping Teva safe?

Panting, Gremory reached down and clasped the slave's cock in her palm. She stroked the hardness. Her claws glistened wickedly from the light off the screen. With her free hand, she crooked a finger to invite a lurking darken over. She smiled and released the slave's cock to allow it to bob. Grabbing the man's thighs, she pulled his legs up to reveal the vulnerable asshole.

"Tempting, isn't it?" Gremory smiled with her order.

The half-demon salivated at the sight. "Yes, mistress."

The slave continued to greedily slurp at Gremory's pussy.

Moloch, one of the Prince's cohorts, thundered into the line of Lash's vision. "Gremory, you lusty cunt, you have lost sight of the punishment here."

"Ah, but the slaves are such fun to play with." She pulled the slave's legs up more and licked his balls. "I only wish I had a real cock to fuck this one with." She rolled her hips.

"I agree. We have to keep the condemned in line. No better way to degrade them than with a hard fuck." Moloch laughed harshly. "I love it when they're so eager to participate. Listen to that one suck at your wet cunt."

She moaned. "So very eager to please me."

Moloch turned to face Lash. "You, slave, haven't pleased anyone."

A shiver raced along his spine as the red eyes bored into his. No, he rarely pleased. At the beginning of his sentence, if a lord had instructed him to sexually please them, he'd done his best. Yet all along, he'd refused to rape or harm another lost soul.

For these reasons, things had never been easy for him in Netherworld. Darkens on their way to turning demon had it light. Turn on another lost soul, and the demons praised you.

And now they expected him to help bring over a free soul. Someone living.

The screen caught his attention.

Teva. She deserved better. Where was her Lord?

"Enough!" Moloch roared, his mouth elongated to that of a

crocodile. His teeth snapped dangerously close to Lash's dangling cock. "Three more deaths!"

His next deaths followed in quick succession. The last the most painful, as he was forced to bleed out until his last drop spilled.

Reviving from his last death, he hit the ground hard and lay still.

On screen, Teva still held him close.

The endless rows of panderers and seducers, forced on by the crack of whips, crawled past.

Nearby on the ground, Gremory held the thighs of the exposed slave while a darken rammed the man's ass. All three moaned, fully enjoying the fuck-fest.

Moloch pulled him up by his hair. "The Prince believes you have it in you to turn Teva to the dark side." His grotesque face pressed too close to Lash's. "Don't dare try any more tricks."

"Yes, master." Lash staggered once the demon lord released his hold.

☙

"Nic!" Teva cried into his ear while cradling him close. She'd collapsed across his chest.

Lash's arms came around her when he was allowed to draw breath once more. Air rushed from his lungs. "Shh..."

"Oh, God." Her head came up to reveal teary eyes. "Nic!"

"Shh."

"You were struck by lightning!" She rubbed his chest. "I saw it! Oh, God..."

He sat up, bringing her up with him. "I'm fine."

She shook her head, clutching his shoulders.

"I'm all right." He caressed her back.

"Oh, God. It was the longest minute of my life." She wiped her eyes.

Yes, what would seem like moments to her would be an eternity to those in Netherworld.

"My damn cell wouldn't work."

"It's okay." He pulled her close to him and groaned when her arms circled his neck.

"I couldn't find your heartbeat." Her arms tightened for only a second, then she pushed back to run her hands over his chest. "I can't believe it. I didn't know what to do. We need to get you to the hospital."

"Shh...I'm fine."

"Let me see how badly you're hurt."

He sucked in a breath when she pushed his t-shirt up, looking for injuries.

"You must have a nasty burn or two." A frown marred her forehead as she searched his chest. Her fingertips roamed over the path her gaze took.

"I'm not hurt."

"You have to have some wound. I saw you get struck."

He caught her hands as his body responded to her nearness as well as her caresses.

She jerked her hands away to pull his shirt down. She rubbed her hands over the cloth. "My God...I swear I thought I saw you get struck by lightning."

"I'm fine, Teva."

"I can't even find a hole in your shirt." She sat back on her ass. "Do you think... Did I imagine it? Did the heat just get to you?" Confusion clouded her expressive eyes.

Having no wish to lie about anything, he lowered his gaze. Let her think what she would. Let her figure out what she could. Through it all, he swore he'd protect her from the legion lords. Never could he bear to see her suffer in Netherworld.

He'd have to do his best to be more careful. Time. He'd need time to figure it all out.

With shaky hands, she pushed her short curls back from her face. "I'm so sorry, I pushed you so hard."

"No." His nostrils flared at the guilt Teva expressed. "I'm fine."

"Let's get you back so you can rest." Teva scrambled up to her knees. "I didn't mean for this to happen."

Lash sighed and lumbered to his feet. He didn't want her to feel to blame, but he didn't know how to fix this.

※

Teva's hands shook as she sliced a tomato.

The scene with Nic wouldn't leave her head. The odd thing was, it seemed to be fading from her memory. She wanted to hang onto as much of it as she could. Maybe she'd caught a glint of sun on his ax? A giant spark of sunlight? She just wasn't sure anymore. He'd collapsed. That much was sure.

Should she force him to visit a hospital? He'd protested in the jeep every time she'd brought up a check-up. It was hard to force someone to do something when they were bigger.

Damn, she should have never allowed him to help. What had she been thinking? Where'd her brain been?

After she cleaned some lettuce, she picked up two bottles. "Mustard or mayo?"

Nic arched an eyebrow. Standing up, he walked over to her. "Either is fine."

"You don't remember which you like best?"

He shook his head.

She set the mayo down and squirted a tiny drop of mustard on her index finger to offer it to his mouth. She sucked in a breath as his tongue scooped up the drop. His tongue was rough and large. Her toes curled. He could offer her so many wicked pleasures.

She repeated the offering with the mayo. Again, she received a jolt of desire from the feel of his tongue on her skin.

Oh...this is a nice treat. She liked his attention, even as simple as it appeared.

"I like them both."

Heat burned her cheeks. "Great." She turned back to the counter. Collecting two slices of deli meats, she faced him once more. "Okay, last choice. Ham or turkey?"

Nic ate first once slice from her fingers, then the other.

The guy had a very fine mouth. She squirmed, waiting to hear his preference.

"Both."

She smiled. God, the guy was easy to please. "Great, go find a seat, and I'll finish lunch."

Picking up his glass, he filled it up with cold water from the fridge. He didn't let the door slam as he went outside.

She sighed. Through the window she watched as he sat under the tree he seemed to like so much.

Never in her life had she been so tempted to break her oath to her mother.

Nic needed protecting. Of that she was sure. Some of her

mother's old spells might help him.

Did she dare dig around in her mom's belongings?

Truth was, her mom had always kept her away from the magic, but right now, she didn't care. Novice or not, she'd seen her mother handle magic all her life. And if it would help Lash, maybe she should try a spell.

Chapter Six

With the football game wrapping up, Teva snuggled close to Nic, as close as she dared. A time or two, she'd wanted to climb into his lap. She enjoyed Nic's rough breathing. Her closeness had turned the big guy on. Moisture heated her sex.

Sweat beaded his upper lip. He raked a hand through his hair as his thigh pressed into hers. A bulge was clearly visible in his pants. Oh yeah, his lap would be the perfect seat.

Watching football was her favorite pastime. It was a hobby she'd shared with her dad and a great annoyance to her mom.

Today, she'd had a real hard time concentrating on the taped game. With the goal of putting the drama of the day behind them, after lunch she'd popped the game in so Nic would relax.

As far as she could tell, he hadn't remembered a thing about the sport.

Odd, because the guy was built like a defensive end, though his grace easily stated quarterback.

So she'd muted the sound and given him her version of the commentary, while she did her best to teach the basics of the sport.

"You thirsty?"

"Yes," he rasped.

Teva reached down into the little cooler and handed him a water bottle. She'd gone all out and brought drinks and snacks to the living room so neither of them would have to get up.

Nic guzzled half his drink before putting the bottle on the coffee table.

It'd been a comfortable lazy afternoon. The only thing that would have beaten it would have been an afternoon of sex. Not a chance of that happening. Though Nic sure didn't seem to mind the closeness, the guy hadn't made a single pass at her.

And she'd gotten a bit frustrated when her team had lost.

She sighed and pressed her upper arm into him.

Purposely, she crossed her legs to draw his attention back to them. His gaze had often lingered on her short-clad thighs, more so than they had the game.

Moisture pooled at the apex of her legs once more. The desire he brought to life fascinated her in a wholly different way. Heat spread up her cheeks as she was tempted to pretend she was a clueless co-ed and throw herself into his arms.

Still, reserve held her back. While intuition told her Nic was interested, his nervousness endeared him to her.

Besides, she was normally not a pursuer where men were concerned. The couple times she'd allowed her hormones to get the best of her—and had taken the initiative—had cost her big time. She'd learned her lesson. If Nic was interested, she wanted him to make the move, at least the first one.

Her thigh brushed his as she shifted. Of course, if he made a sexual advance toward her...she'd eagerly welcome his touch. Yes, another risk was in her future.

Nic straightened at the knock on the front door.

Teva hated to see the pleasant afternoon end. "I'm not expecting anyone." With a sigh, she got up and moved toward the door. Looking outside, she groaned. "Oh, damn." She peeked outside again. *Damn.* Her aunt. Of all people. She hadn't seen Clarisse since her parents' deaths. Not a single form of communication had passed between them since the funerals.

Teva wasn't close to the woman. Her mom hadn't even been close to the woman. The two women had been like day and night. What could Clarisse want now? Other than to make Teva miserable, which her aunt always seemed to do when she appeared.

Quickly, she ran her hands through her curls and rolled her eyes at her outfit. No time to change or hide.

Nic frowned, no doubt concerned with the change in her body language.

"It's my aunt. Don't let her get to you," she told herself more than him.

He nodded as she pulled open the door to allow Clarisse to enter.

"Nic, this is my aunt, Clarisse." Teva waved a hand between them. "Clarisse, Nic." Nervously, Teva rubbed her hands on her shorts.

"Hello, Teva." Clarisse breezed inside, looking like a million bucks. God, the woman *never* aged. Older than her deceased mother, Clarisse had to be nearing seventy, but she looked no more than thirty. Not a single gray hair showed in her thick, long auburn locks either.

Always a little uncomfortable around the woman, Teva sighed. Clarisse would make a New York fashion model look drab. Though Nic looked just as gorgeous.

She folded her arms, wishing she'd had time to primp.

"Hello, Clarisse." He moved closer to place Teva within his personal space and clasped Teva's right shoulder. She leaned back into his chest. She wasn't beyond taking what little comfort he could give. His ability to sense her rising distress somehow calmed her nerves.

"You know to call me Darkraven." Clarisse gave Teva a sharp look.

Teva caught her lip between her teeth. Nothing would make her call her aunt by her chosen priestess name. Not even her mom had belonged to her aunt's coven.

Clarisse turned a false smile toward Nic. "Hello, Nic. You look cozy with my niece." The immaculately dressed woman walked past them toward the eating table. "First time I've ever discovered a man out here."

Teva tensed under his palm. Her aunt's comment hit a nerve. How would the woman know who she had for company? Clarisse never visited.

Please don't let Clarisse start now. Not in front of Nic.

"Please ignore her," Teva mouthed, as she moved to her aunt's side. "Would you like some tea?"

"Oh, that would be heavenly. It was a long drive out here." Clarisse settled onto a chair. She folded her manicured hands on the tabletop. "I've missed you, dear. I've been worried about you living out here alone."

"My cabins have visitors all the time. I'm rarely alone." With a toss of her hair, Teva moved off into the kitchen. Over her shoulder, she saw Nic sit across from Clarisse.

Bless him.

"Not the same, dear. We're family."

She rushed getting drinks poured.

Maybe things would go smoothly. He could have gone outside and sat under the tree he liked, if Clarisse had made him feel as uncomfortable as Teva felt. She'd never told her mom, but she hadn't cared for her aunt since she'd been a freshman in high school. Something about Clarisse had changed back then. Soured the woman somehow. Teva had never been able to pinpoint the change, but still it remained below the surface.

"So, Nic, tell me about yourself. And my niece."

He shifted.

Teva placed a glass of tea in front of Clarisse and the second in front of Nic. "Not much to tell. We met. Got along and were spending an afternoon together." She slid into a chair cattycorner to both of them.

"I see." Clarisse sipped her brew.

Teva's back teeth ground together hard enough to jumpstart an ache in her jaw. "So, what prompted this visit?"

Clarisse's wide-set eyes were shielded by long, thick lashes. "It has been a while since we've had a visit. I thought it my place to check on you."

Teva bit back a snort. Her aunt hadn't even put in an appearance at the meal after her parents' funerals. There hadn't been a single call between them since. Though Teva supposed her aunt wasn't entirely to blame. Teva never sought the older woman out, either.

She stared at the narrow flawless face so much like her mom's. Still, something niggled her nerves with Clarisse. Her aunt wanted something—just what, Teva couldn't guess.

"How's the rental business?" Her aunt swept a lock of hair over her shoulder.

Teva continued to clench her teeth. She had more than a rental business. She lived on her parents' land preserve. She released a calming breath. "Busy, and how's your coven?"

"We've thrived. I'm so fortunate to have my sisters and

brothers."

A shiver hit Teva's spine. She didn't know much about her aunt's coven, but she knew her mom hadn't accepted the beliefs. Once upon a time, Clarisse had tried to recruit Teva's mom.

"I battled some depression just after..." Clarisse swallowed. "But I've coped. How about you? The loneliness must be harder on you. After all, I do have my coven to rely on."

Of course, she'd suffered some depression. She'd gone through all the stages of grief since she'd learned how her parents had lost their lives. A storm. Slick roads. And a semi truck had stolen something precious to her. Her parents had been such a big part of her life. "I'm fine."

"You look as if you've gained some weight..." After delivering the barb, Clarisse took a drink of her tea. "Dear, you can't let food compensate for the loneliness."

Teva stiffened. In her teen years, her weight had always seesawed. And still today, she always tried to be careful when it came to sweets. She'd never been thin like Clarisse and her mom. "Healthy" was how she described herself. It'd have been nice to blame her father's genes, but he'd never had weight issues. "I weigh no more than I did the last time you saw me."

"Of course, dear. This old memory of mine." Clarisse patted Teva's hand with a clammy palm. "You do know if you ever need me for anything...I am here for you."

Teva met her aunt's gaze. No compassion gleamed from the emerald depths. She sighed. Clarisse was so different from her mom.

After another drink, her aunt stood up with a purse in hand. "If you'll excuse me, I need to use the bathroom."

"Sure." Teva waved a hand. Clarisse knew where everything was located. Teva lived in what had been her parents' home.

Odd. Teva watched as Clarisse bypassed the guest bathroom down the hall and went inside her own bedroom and closed the door.

Had Nic left the seat up? She doubted it. She'd never spent time with a more careful man.

"You all right?" Nic reached out and caressed her fingertips.

"Oh." Desire sparked low in her stomach. "Yeah. We're not close."

He nodded.

"You don't have to sit through this…"

The slightest of grins touched his lips. "I don't mind."

Teva's heart thumped a mad pace.

God, the guy is gorgeous.

"Maybe we can go out to dinner to make up for this?"

"I'm fine." He shrugged. "Dinner here will be just fine."

Disappointment slumped her shoulders. She wouldn't have minded going out with him somewhere.

"You're a good cook. I've enjoyed your meals so far."

She sighed happily at his praise. Wowza…she could get used to him. And nothing wrong with staying in. Quite cozy, actually.

Clarisse joined them once more and placed her purse in a free chair.

The next few minutes filled with small talk, sprinkled with the occasional discreet jab at Teva's lack of pizzazz and flair.

Teva did her best to ignore the remarks. She worked hard and loved her life; what did her dress matter?

Through the conversation, Nic remained silent.

Finally, Clarisse stood. "Well, I hate to run, but I've got plans this evening. I'll be late getting back as it is."

Teva couldn't stand up quickly enough to see her out.

She frowned. Clarisse moved to Nic's side when he stood as well. Rising up on tiptoes, the older woman kissed Nic's cheek and embraced him, her hands roaming over his shoulders.

Nic didn't break eye contact with her over her aunt's head.

Teva looked down. She'd never seen her aunt so affectionate with anyone before.

Yes, Clarisse was up to something.

At the door, her aunt gave her a mock hug. "I'll be in touch."

"Drive safe."

"Oh, don't worry about me." An eerie smile flashed across Clarisse's face.

Teva shivered.

☙

Lash ran a hand through his hair and glanced at Teva's bedroom door. She'd closed it, partly because she'd gone to soak in a tub. She'd said as much before she'd disappeared.

Teva had needed some space after their unwelcome visitor. She'd escaped moments after Clarisse had left.

Good riddance. As much as he knew the thought was wrong, he couldn't ask forgiveness.

The look Clarisse had sent him before her impulsive kiss told him, she knew something he didn't. It had been a very long time since anyone had unnerved him so.

The hair on his arms had stood up on end when he'd seen her expression. The woman was no good. He couldn't put his finger on it, but he'd spent far too long with evil not to know *bad* when he met it.

Teva's aunt had a place waiting for her in Netherworld.

Dread kept him tense. Pushing to his feet, he paced. He wanted to protect her. Needed to. No inspiration hit as he walked from one end of the room to the other.

Maybe Clarisse wouldn't make any more appearances.

There was always hope, at least, for those who still walked among the living.

Lash turned at the sound of the door opening. His breath quickened. The response never failed. She took his breath away. Each time he saw her, it was like the first time all over again. Her beauty would preserve him for the rest of his eternity.

"Hey, I feel better now."

He nodded. She looked delectable with her damp hair and skin. She wore another pair of short pants. He enjoyed looking at her naked thighs as much as he liked gazing at the cleavage of her exposed breasts. Even her arms gained his attention in her sleeveless shirt. She looked so soft with all her curves.

The front of his jeans tightened at the expansion of his cock. With another breath, it swelled rigid.

Under his gaze, her nipples pebbled beneath the thin cloth she wore.

Lust ran hot in his veins. Sweat beaded his palms.

The pleasure of sex was within his reach, if he only dared risk the repercussions. If he took her, he could taint her. No. He wouldn't risk that. Even knowing her touch could erase all the pain he'd suffered didn't hold enough temptation to bring him to do her harm.

Not wishing to make her uncomfortable, he looked away.

"I'm sorry about." She waved her hand. "Clarisse..."

"She makes you uncomfortable?" He held his breath and

waited for some attack from Netherworld.

Suspicion rose up along with the hair on the back of his neck. What if Clarisse was part of Teva's demise?

No. The betrayal of a family member would be too much. Such betrayal was an uncommon occurrence among his people, yet he'd witnessed too much in Netherworld. Clarisse's evilness could delve that low.

Her brow creased with a frown, showing him the trouble she carried. "Oh, we've never been close. Have you ever had family you didn't really know? Or care much about?" She settled onto the couch, tucking a foot under her ass.

Two strides placed him at the other end. He sat so he could turn to face her. "My family was a small one. But, yes, I've known many I've not cared about." The list of demons and darkens who'd tormented him scrolled endlessly in his mind. "Family or not, people are people." He shrugged. "We don't choose our family."

His chest constricted at the sight of tears welling in her eyes.

"I know it's wrong, but sometimes I wonder why my parents...and not her..." Her mouth trembled as more tears pooled.

"Don't cry, Teva." Without hesitation, he scooped her up into his lap.

Willingly, she wrapped her arms around his neck.

Both her nearness and the emotions she evoked made it difficult to breathe. He cradled her to his chest and caressed her back. "Shh."

"I know it's so wrong." She hugged him tightly.

"Shh...it's our actions that harm others. Not our wants or wishes. I'm sure many have felt the same." He cupped the back of her head in his hand, his fingers tangled in her curls. He wanted nothing more than to ease her pain. "I'm sorry for your loss."

"Will it ever get easier?" She sniffled into his ear.

"Yes. One day you'll see them again in the Afterworld."

He closed his eyes to risk a prayer.

Lord, let it be so.

A soft breath heated his neck. "Thank you, Nic." She sat up and wiped her eyes. "I swear, I don't normally fall apart like this."

With a thumb, he caught a stray tear. "We all have our moments."

She smiled gently. "I bet you haven't."

A side of his mouth turned up in response.

If she only knew. He'd cried like a toddler when he'd awakened that first time in Netherworld. His first few tortured deaths had him begging for mercy, though he'd grown used to the agony soon enough. There was no pity to be found in Netherworld. At least not from those who wielded the power.

He rubbed her arms in a soothing motion. "You okay?"

She nodded and sighed before she left his lap.

Already, he missed her closeness.

"How about I put some gumbo on for dinner?"

Never having heard of gumbo, he nodded. As long as there was plenty of water, he didn't care what he ate.

ଔ

Lash stood under the warm, pelting water. He tilted his head back and let the shower wash away the grime of the day, along with his impure thoughts.

He wanted Teva more with every moment he spent in her company.

His now-heavy cock pulsed, not paying his will any mind.

Private showers. What an incredible invention. In Netherworld there was never any privacy. Demon lords hounded over you while darkens continuously taunted everyone. Here with Teva, he enjoyed showers very much. In Netherworld, the closest to a shower you got was when the skin was boiled from your body.

In Netherworld, he'd never been permitted pleasure. Only degradation, pain, and shame.

Seeking a moment of pleasure, he grasped his cock with an image of Teva in mind. She'd be so warm and soft in his arms. So needy. Never had he consoled anyone before. He'd never been needed before.

His soapy hand ran along the hard length.

The air shifting behind him warned him he was no longer alone. The accompanying stink left no doubt. He stilled at the feel of a female body pressing into his back. He didn't have to open his eyes to know it wasn't Teva.

"Hello, Lash." Gremory's sultry voice hummed in his ear.

"Mistress."

"Moloch says I need to make up for shirking my duty on your last visit home." She clasped his shoulders, her claws dangerously tight. "We think you need some sweet bribery to complete your task."

Abruptly, the shower stall closed in as they were joined by another.

Gremory sucked in a breath and dropped her hands. If room had allowed, the demoness would've dropped to her knees in as much fear as show of respect.

Lash kept his eyes downcast. No one dared to look into the eyes of their Prince.

"Go home, Gremory." A sneer was clear in the dark lord's tone. "Wait in my chamber for punishment."

Lash risked a glance up at his Prince. He'd only been in his presence a time or two. Everyone feared being called out by the Prince. Today, he'd shifted into a blond male, which was no doubt how he'd once appeared as a fallen angel.

"Yes, my lord." Gremory disappeared on a whimper.

The Prince sighed. "It seems many of my disciples believe I've chosen poorly." A shiver ran up Lash's body as the Prince clasped the side of his face and forced him to meet cruel demon eyes. "But I think not. And do you know why that is, slave?"

"No, my lord." Lash swallowed, mesmerized by the fire blazing in the demon lord's eyes.

"I'll get far too much pleasure out of eating you and shitting you out." A twisted smile crossed the Prince's mouth. "Just to do it again."

Lash's heart hammered. The Prince's words had been more than an idle threat. Never had he believed someone more.

"I'll never let a soul due me escape. You will bring Teva to our side." The Prince nuzzled Lash's temple. "Fuck her. Get her to break any number of sins. Just remember, she mustn't repent before her death. That doesn't seem like too difficult a task for one with your masculine beauty."

Lash forced a nod.

"Nicodemus, do you know why I singled you out?"

Again, the Prince forced him to meet his burning gaze.

"Because you never broke. You simply accepted your fate."

Lash closed his eyes. Yes, he'd accepted his place in

Netherworld.

"I think bringing you back home after you complete this for me...will be pure torture on your already lost soul. After all, I'm giving you all this...to remember." The Prince's twisted smile was back.

Lash's chest constricted at the sickening thought of the inevitable.

"Now, I must go home and punish several for interfering with your task." The Prince patted Lash's cheek. "Slave, you have my word, you'll have no more visits. You'll be free to play house to your heart's content."

"Yes, my Prince."

The Prince eased back a half of a step. "But remember, I do have the power to control you. In no time, I'll hold Teva's future in my hands. In Netherworld, I can offer her a life of leisure." Then, without another word, he disappeared.

Life of leisure meant you winded up in the Prince's harem. Sickness knotted his stomach. Teva didn't belong in Netherworld at all, let alone at the feet of the Prince.

Turning the water hotter, Lash sat on the floor of the stall.

He'd just been paid a visit by Satan.

Chapter Seven

"Teva?" A murmur burred into her sleep-dulled mind, followed by a low buzz.

Oh, yes. Nic's knee-weakening voice. She rolled over to bring her legs up. Liquid heat pooled from her sex.

Nic was there with her...his hand reached down to touch... Soon, he'd part her legs and put his big body between her thighs to thrust deep...

"Teva?" The touch wasn't where she wanted the sensation.

She moaned.

"Teva?"

She stretched under the pressure on her shoulder and jerked to full alertness. She sat up and stared at Nic. The alarm buzzer continued to hum.

Well, heck and damn.

Just a dream.

"I didn't know what the sound meant." He raked a hand through his tousled hair. "It sounded, then stopped many times."

The snooze button. She was in the habit of hitting it a dozen or more times, especially when overtired. They'd stayed up until the early morning hours watching cartoons. Nic had been enthralled with the characters, and she was glad her parents had held onto her old collection. She'd enjoyed watching the classics as much as she'd liked watching Nic munch handfuls of the popcorn she'd popped.

She'd never seen Nic as animated as he was while watching the shows, so she'd promised they would watch more of them later. She had dozens to pick from.

Quickly, she reached out and pressed the button to turn the alarm off. "Sorry I woke you. I have to give a camper a key early this morning." No way had she wanted to end their fun. But toothpicks wouldn't have kept her eyes open any longer when she'd finally called it a night.

Through her lashes, she let her gaze roam down Nic's muscular body. Broad chest. Twelve pack. And a hard-on presented so temptingly beneath the boxer-briefs he wore.

His cock was thick and long. It ran up toward his right hip under the gray material.

She licked her lips. What a way to wake up. She'd never been so thankful for someone's lack of modesty before. Nic simply didn't care about his nakedness. Walking by last night, his door had been wide open, and he had stripped as she'd passed. She'd not only peeked, but had turned her head to watch. He must sleep naked.

He probably wouldn't be wearing anything now, if she hadn't suggested he not walk around completely naked.

Silly Teva. She still kicked herself for the suggestion.

His hands fisted.

Teva looked up to be captivated by his hooded gaze.

She sucked in a breath as her barely concealed nipples puckered under a light tank top. Liquid heat lit in her clit.

How easy it would be for her to pull the band of his shorts down to reveal his erection.

Do it...

Be wild...

Thrill him...

She gasped at the echoing voices.

It would be so easy.

So welcomed...

Look at him...

Desire heated as she did just that. She looked her fill.

Sheen of sweat already covers him...

Don't think, just act.

Her clit pulsed in encouragement.

It would be easy.

Teva reached out and grasped his hips.

Nic caught her hands. "Teva..." His thick lashes lowered to shield his black eyes.

Desire shone in his hooded gaze and in the tension of his body. He wanted her.

She scrambled up onto her knees. Her hipsters tightened along her crotch to rub deliciously along her clit.

His large hands gripped her smaller ones. "You said you needed...the key..."

Reluctantly, she glanced at the clock and groaned. *No time.* She'd hit the snooze for over an hour. No wonder Nic had gotten concerned.

She sat back on her butt to rake her hands through her hair.

Damn, what had come over her?

Nic walked away.

Teva jumped off the bed at the sight on his back. "God, Nic, your...your mark..."

He glanced back over a shoulder.

"It looks so painful." She moved toward him for a closer look. The mark looked burned, as if...

"It's nothing." He walked away, but she followed.

Inside the room where he'd been sleeping, he pulled a t-shirt from a drawer and put it on with quick motions. Next, he removed his shorts and slid into a pair of jeans. Teva got distracted as he worked to get his big cock tucked away.

Lord, he was fine.

He winced as he buttoned his jeans. "I'll pour you some juice and heat a pastry you like for breakfast." The shorts, he folded neatly and placed on the corner of the dresser.

Always so neat.

She caressed his arm to stop him. "Please Nic, let me see your back. I can at least put some antibiotic ointment on it."

"I'll not let you touch what's on my back." A tic popped to life in his clenched jaw.

She rubbed his arm. She'd never seen him so angry before. "I want to help you."

"Forget it's there."

Teva stepped back. "Fine, but I want you to tend to the wound. It's high on your shoulder. You can reach it yourself."

He nodded and followed her to the bathroom. When she pulled down some first aid ointment, she remembered some cream. Her mom had been given a special medication for a burn from a pressure cooker.

She scrambled down under the sink until she located the jar. Quickly, she checked the expiration date before she straightened up. In a flash, she opened the lid. She scooped some cream onto a Q-tip. "Here you go. Rub it all around.

There's plenty more."

Nic removed half his t-shirt while she got the medicine ready.

Eyes closed, he did as she instructed.

While his back was turned to her, she viewed the mark in the mirror. He must have forgotten about mirror being there. So many things were new to him...like the cartoons everyone should have seen. Or at least one of them.

The mirror allowed her to see the eye held an angry-looking burn now. The wound hadn't been there before...not before the incident in the woods. She'd nearly convinced herself nothing had happened. But now, looking at this, she knew better.

Nic had been hurt that day.

Though the wound looked painful, his facial expression revealed nothing as he finished the task.

"I hope it doesn't hurt."

"It's nothing."

"If it doesn't heal, we can have a doctor look at it. For now, apply this three times a day."

"It's not worth the trouble."

Once done, she put the medicine up while he washed his hands. "Thank you, Nic. I'll feel better about it since we've at least put something on it."

He slung his arm back through the hole. "I'll go get you something to eat for breakfast." He didn't look her in the eye before heading to the kitchen.

She sighed and closed the door.

Nic needed her help. Her intuition was clear on the matter. And now her concerns had intensified at the sight of the bloody burned eye on his back

☙

Teva pushed the buggy along the grocery aisle. She couldn't put the chore off any longer. Nic had a big appetite and her stores had been depleted. Truth was, she normally didn't eat well, but with Nic around, she'd been making meals.

After dropping the key off to a new visitor they'd headed into town and the local grocery store.

Food. Nic was enthralled by all the different food groups. Now he sniffed a kiwi.

She curled her nose. "They're rather sour."

He inhaled again. "I like the smell of fruits."

That'd been easy to tell, since they'd now spent twenty minutes in the produce section as he got a whiff of all the different varieties.

A pretty blonde moved up, standing too close to Nic as she inspected a papaya.

Teva looked away. This wasn't the first time a woman had gotten too close to Nic inside the store. Though Nic's lack of flirting impressed her, the other woman's nearness bothered her.

"What do you think of this one? Too ripe?" The blonde offered Nic the papaya.

He put the kiwi back. "I wouldn't know, mistress." Two steps brought him to Teva's side.

The blonde's wide eyes followed his movements.

She sighed. God, she was being juvenile again. Nic appeared not to notice the games the ladies had been playing with him. His lack of reaction fascinated her. Where had he been all this time? How could he have forgotten so much?

Teva collected several fruits, including a kiwi and papaya for Nic to have later. They moved on. In the cereal aisle, a woman asked him to get a box from the top shelf. Teva refrained from rolling her eyes. The woman was taller than she was.

Jealousy was a new experience for Teva. Worst part, Nic was nothing to her. Only a guy she was helping out.

She sighed and moved on to another aisle. A woman on a cell phone turned her head all the way around to gawk at Nic.

He kept walking to examine packages. Anything that caught his interest, she put into the cart.

Yeah, she was probably spoiling him. But so what? It was fun.

While she got the cleaning supplies she needed, Nic picked up a toy an infant tossed down twice. The exchange made her notice a part of herself that had never existed before.

God, she was in trouble if a baby was getting to her.

Nic didn't speak to the child, simply handed the toy back to the mother.

Teva moved on, and Nic followed right behind.

They turned on to the row of milk, and she couldn't stop the question. "Nic, do you have children, or think you have children?" She swallowed. "A wife?"

He stopped walking, forcing her to do the same. "No, Teva, I don't." His voice sounded strong and sure.

It was the most certain she'd ever heard him. "How can you be so sure?" She shifted uncomfortably. "I mean you've been...things have seemed so new to you."

"I've never known... A wife, I'd remember."

A bit flabbergasted, she stared.

"I'm a virgin, Teva." He looked completely serious.

No way. He was far too fine.

"I do not lie."

A warmth fluttered low in her belly. Something about Nic ignited her belief.

She nodded. "Great. That's cool. I mean, I've heard of those who abstain." Though she'd never considered the idea too closely herself. Had always assumed those who did so were religious. She didn't get that impression from Nic. So maybe she'd been way off on all counts.

Wow. She pushed the buggy forward to collect some eggs and butter before placing two gallons of milk into the cart.

A virgin. What had possessed him to hold off on sex?

Her mind remained occupied with images from the morning when they strolled up to a checkout lane. She'd nearly given him head earlier. Heat warmed her cheeks.

With a turn of her head, she scanned the magazines and newspapers. Anything to take her mind off the loss of swallowing for him. At least now she understood his reserve…

Teva's heart pounded at the sight of the car crash on the front page of the local paper. With a trembling hand, she picked up the paper to read.

"What is it?" Nic stepped into her personal space.

In disbelief, she reread. Jenna Holliard, age thirty-three, had died in a fiery automobile crash.

Stunned, she looked up to meet Nic's black gaze.

"Jenna's gone. She died in a car wreck."

"I'm sorry, Teva."

She swallowed. She hadn't known Jenna that well, only as an acquaintance, but still—to have seen someone only days before, then to find out they'd died…

She glanced at the article again to find the location of the accident. Then her eyes flew to the date of the crash...

Dear God, Jenna might have been driving home from her visit with them when she'd died.

○○

Lash carried in the last of the bags and placed them on the table. He urged Teva to leave the chore for him. "I can deal with this." He shifted to pull out items. "I know you want to find out more about Jenna."

On the drive home, they'd been quiet except for Teva saying she'd check online to see if she could find out more. She'd also explained about online. Or at least tried to. The Internet was a place he didn't understand.

"You sure?"

"Yes. Go look for what you need." He wanted to hold her, but managed to refrain. Learning of Jenna's death had shaken Teva up. He'd seen it in her eyes. And even though fate had willed Jenna's passing, he still felt partly to blame.

"Thanks." With slumped shoulders, Teva went to the computer near the television in the corner.

The chore of putting the food away wasn't much of a task. Not even a tedious one, though the more he pulled from the bags, the more his agitation built.

Teva had paid for all this. Bags and bags full of food.

He could remember his old life. The Olympian hopefuls had demanded much of their gems and gold, so they'd bartered among themselves to get what they needed. Food. Clothes. Weapons.

Earlier, the man had paid Teva for the use of her cabin.

And then she'd paid for the groceries.

Lash had no money to offer.

This bothered him greatly.

He put everything neatly away, including the bags. Teva remained on the computer as he sat on the couch.

After another minute or two, she swung her chair around. "I'd like for us to go to her viewing."

Unsure of what a viewing was, he tilted his head.

"Well, *I* need to go to the viewing." She pulled a leg up and wrapped her arms around her folded knee. "I'd like for you to go with me."

"I don't remember what a viewing is."

"Oh, the viewing is a time where friends, family and acquaintances can pay their respects to Jenna and her family."

He nodded.

"It's held a time or two before a funeral. It can give those unable or unwilling to attend the funeral a chance to say goodbye."

Again, he nodded. "And a funeral?"

Her blue eyes widened. "A funeral is a burial. Or, in some cases, a cremated body is displayed in a urn, and last words are spoken over the body."

Ah...he'd had burials in his time. His people were burned after death. Unsure, he looked away. He wanted to do anything Teva asked, but his kind were condemned and weren't permitted on holy ground. Or so an ancient lost soul had told him. Did a viewing take place on sacred ground? Would he be able to tell before he stepped upon it? He had no wish to frighten Teva again. Yet he dared not ask her too many questions.

"I didn't know Jenna."

She sighed. "I know...it's okay. I'll go alone."

He swallowed. He couldn't be the reason she looked so lost. "I'll go with you."

She lifted her gaze. "Are you sure?"

He nodded. At worst, all that could happen would be the ground swallowing him up. He'd been ingested by many things before. "Yes, we'll go together."

"Great." She spun around to her computer again. After a second, she stood up. "Okay. We'll need to get you a nice set of dressier clothes."

He balked. Clothes meant more payment to acquire. "I have clothes." She'd even taught him to wash them properly.

"Oh, I know, but we'll need to dress a bit more formally."

"Teva..." He lowered his gaze. In his time, he'd been prosperous. In this world, he didn't know how to get by. Even in Netherworld, he'd survived through his eternity of deaths without owing anyone a thing. "I don't wish to burden you further."

"Oh, no. It's fine. One day, when you remember who you are..."

"I'm Nicodemus."

Teva edged to his side and eased down onto the couch. "I know, and one day you'll remember everything."

His lashes lowered. To some, omission was as much of a lie as speaking a falsehood aloud. There wasn't a moment of his life, or deaths, he couldn't recall. Little of it could be shared.

"Hey, don't worry about this. You're doing me a favor by going with me. I've always hated these things." Her curls bounced as she shook her head. "I can't explain it. I've not gone to many of these. Only my parents' and an uncle's when I was a little girl. I just don't want to go alone."

"I'll go with you."

There had been no real choice.

Chapter Eight

Teva scampered into the storage room at the end of the hallway. The room had once been her parents' master bedroom, but now only contained her parents' old belongings. Though she'd already claimed a few keepsakes, she'd yet to be able to go through everything and donate what was usable.

The morning and early afternoon had gone by quickly as she and Nic had cleaned cabins up for new arrivals. Nic was a great help. The work hadn't been so bad with him around.

Now she wanted to find her Mom's old spell book before she had to shower. They had maybe two hours before they had to leave for Jenna's viewing.

No easy task. In her grief, she'd simply boxed up most of their belongings and sealed the cardboard closed with masking tape.

For a while, she opened boxes and resealed them when she didn't find what she was looking for. Where would she have put her mother's craft material? Did she even put it all together?

"Teva?"

On a gasp, she straightened up from where she'd been kneeling.

"I didn't mean to startle you."

Feeling a little silly, she smiled. "Hey, you."

"What are you doing?"

"I'm just looking for something."

"What is it? I can help look."

Regarding the cartons, she shrugged. "I'm looking for a special journal of my mom's."

"Ah..." The tiniest of smiles tipped up the corner of his mouth.

The smile jumpstarted her desire. Pleasant sensations hummed low in her belly.

"And a journal would look like?"

"Oh." She laughed and held up her hands to show him. "It's about this long and..." She shifted her hands. "This wide. It's kind of bulky, overflowing with stuff."

He nodded. "Stuff."

Lower lip caught between her teeth, she studied Nic as he collected one of the knives she had to open a box. How did one explain magic to someone who couldn't recall his last name? Dare she risk a confrontation? Not everyone was open-minded.

Her parents had learned that the hard way. It happened to be one of the two reasons her mom had asked her to leave the family gift alone. She still didn't understand the other reason she'd been asked to reject magic.

Out of respect for her parents, she'd ignored what had been so important to them, but now...she wanted to see if there was any way to help Nic.

Surely they'd understand her reasoning.

"I found something that might be a journal." Near the closet, Nic held up a photo album. "There are a few journals here."

"Oh, hey." She hobbled over boxes to get to his side. Accepting the book, she plunked down on a bare spot on a chest of drawers. "These are family photo albums." She smiled as he moved closer. "But you've got the general idea of a journal."

Sitting Indian-style, she opened the book to reveal family memories. Nic folded his arms and placed a hip near her knee. The atmosphere was cozy as she talked of her childhood. Most of the pictures were of her, she explained, flipping through the images. Holidays. Birthday parties. Year after year of school pictures.

Ugh. She tried to cover her freshman picture from high school, but Nic removed her hand.

"I looked hideous." Pudgy and dotted with acne. She shuddered. He'd probably never been fat or suffered a blemish.

"You do not. Only young."

She snorted. High school years hadn't been kind. She'd enjoyed college so much more, especially when she'd gone for her master's.

He passed her a second album.

"This one's great. Vacations. Dad loved amusement parks. Football games and roller coasters were his hobbies."

Nic grunted, looking at the gigantic roller coaster behind her and her dad.

"Nothing beat the thrill of an adrenaline rush for Dad. We traveled to a different amusement park every single year."

"You look like your mother."

She gazed up from the page to meet Nic's black eyes. "Yeah, but I always thought she was much prettier."

He gently tugged on one of her curls. "You are lovely."

Teva lowered her gaze as heat spread up her neck and cheeks. He'd looked sincere. Yet anyone could see her Mom far surpassed her in looks.

"Same eyes. Skin tone. Vibrant hair. You are much alike."

"I guess." She sighed and flipped the page.

"I speak only the truth. You're lovely and look like your mother."

She smiled. "Okay, I guess I resemble her." She released a heavy breath. "Just wish she were here so we could do girl stuff again."

"Ah." A grin curled his mouth up. It was a tempting sight. She loved to see his barely-there smiles. "Girl stuff?"

"Yeah, you know, day spa trips. Fixing up each other's hair. Shopping for shoes…Getting our nails and toenails painted…"

"Ah." He nodded. "Girl stuff. I won't do those things with you."

She laughed.

"Not even if you say please." His grin grew.

"Oh my gosh, Nic…" She laughed harder until she had to wipe her eyes dry. She could get used to him teasing. "Thank you." She placed her hand on his shoulder. "I appreciate the company."

Bone and muscle played under her palm, so she let him go. He shifted away. "Do you want another album?"

"Nope, I'll look through more later. I still want to find the journal before we have to leave." Sliding off the chest, she placed the books inside the box and yelped. A huge spider crawled along outside of the bottom of the box. Her heart thumped. She didn't mind snakes or alligators, but spiders gave her the willies.

Frantic, she took her shoe off to smack it before it got away.

Nic's hand clasped her arm mid-swing. "No."

"Huh?" She looked between the gigantic spider and Nic.

"It's an enormous spider."

Thick lashes lowered to shield his gaze. "I've heard it told, you're not to kill living creatures."

Her nose curled. "It's a spider. That would more than likely bite one of us..."

"You ever hear tell of myths? Superstitions?"

"Yes." He had her full attention. Witchcraft relied heavily on people's beliefs. Sympathetic magic and such.

"Legends speak of people being cursed inside living things. Spiders. Rats. Trees. And if you purposely kill them..."

Her eyes narrowed on the monstrous spider that now rested on a corner of the cardboard. "Are you saying you don't kill bugs?"

"Not knowingly."

"Even if I say please?" She gave a pouty look that had always worked on her Dad.

"Don't give me that look." A smile tipped the right corner of his mouth up.

As tempted as she was to lick her lips at his appeal, she continued to pout. Heck and damn. She didn't like spiders. Never had.

"What if I take it outside? I could release it out there."

She gasped.

"I can take it far away from the house."

A shiver ran up her spine. Hold a spider? Yuck! Not her. Not a chance. At least snakes were beautiful, with the skin designs. So smooth to the touch. But a spider? Just plain creepy. "You do what you have to do. I'll go stand over there while you do your thing." She scrambled to the other side of the room where she'd been when he'd entered.

Suspiciously, she eyed him. She could recall a time or two when her dad had told her mom he was going to get rid of a spider, but wasn't quick enough and the nasty thing had gotten away. Teva had been sworn to secrecy so her mom wouldn't have a tizzy over living with a spider. Teva's own fear hadn't developed until college, when she'd stepped on a spider's egg nest. Tiny spiders had swarmed her body. Never since had she been so freaked.

Her skin crawled at the memory.

From the hallway, she listened to Nic as he murmured to the spider.

Helplessly, she followed to the front window of the house to watch Nic take the spider some distance away from the house. He was entirely too comfortable with the creepy thing. But with Nic's belief in the myth, maybe he'd understand her need in experimenting with her mom's spells. There might very well be something in her mom's notes to help him without a trip to a hospital.

It was worth a shot.

An antique clock chimed the hour. She sighed and headed toward the shower.

Finding the spell book would have to wait.

෦෩

Lash tugged at his neckline once more, trying to loosen the thing called a tie Teva had made him wear. No, a tie didn't compare to the agony of a chain, whip, or even a boa constrictor wrapped around one's throat, yet he'd prefer not to be wearing one. Then again, a tie did remind him of a collar some demon lords forced the condemned to wear.

He ran two fingers between the cloth and his skin. Ties were uncomfortable things. It was a wonder the living didn't ban them.

"Don't worry. You look great." Teva smiled before she backed her car into a spot and parked.

Letting go of his shirt, he grunted. The tie wasn't a cause for worry. He just didn't understand why he had to bother with the neck cloth or nicer clothes. The dress pants Teva had picked out didn't hide his erection nearly as well as jeans. And his boots were more comfortable than the shoes he now wore.

She ran her hands through her curls while she looked into the little mirror. She glanced his way. "You really do look great." A flush spread across her cheeks.

His cock sprang to life once more. With another rush of desire, his hard-on filled up the front of his pants. The fact Teva was about to say goodbye to Jenna did nothing to cool his lust. "You're lovely, Teva."

"Thank you."

He particularly enjoyed the way her new dress clung to her breasts.

"Okay, let's go on in. Hopefully, we've missed most of the crowd." She pushed her door open and stepped out without another word.

Reluctantly, he followed. Teva came around the auto to his side. Her arm brushed his. Her nearness calmed him. "Since we've yet to figure out your last name, I'm going to continue to introduce you as Nic Lash."

He nodded. *Nic Lash.* Easy for him to remember. He'd already become accustomed to Teva calling him Nic.

The closer they got to the building, the more he shortened his strides. Did the funeral home rest on sacred ground? Would it swallow him whole if he stepped inside? Would electricity strike him down? Only this time would the bolt be hurtled from the Afterworld? Would his attempt at entering a sacred building anger those that ruled the Afterworld?

He had no wish to anger the heavenly beings. He had enough to worry about with those Netherworld-bound.

"Hey, it's okay." Teva squeezed his arm. "Why don't you hang out here a few minutes?"

A relieved breath rushed from his lungs. "Thank you." Guilt at allowing Teva to go in alone thundered its way into his chest. Yet she was probably safer with him outside.

She turned her head, and her curls bounced. "Can you remember the name of Jenna's cousin she mentioned? I thought I'd see if she was here."

Lash glanced up at the sky. Would he be struck down for helping her remember? "Ally Cease." His body relaxed when no torture was forthcoming.

"Oh, great." She smiled teasingly. "If I get desperate, I'll come find you."

After the door closed behind her, he braced a shoulder against a pole. It wasn't so bad out here at all. Although Teva had commented the crowd might have thinned out by now, many cars filled the parking lot and lined the street.

"Hello, mister." An elderly black man approached him.

He nodded to the man.

The man extended his hand. "Reverend Powell."

"Nic Lash." He was thankful he'd gone through this routine with the camper who'd rented Teva's cabin yesterday.

"Good to know you."

"Same here." After a firm grip, Lash released the man's hand.

"Tell me, Nic Lash, do you see someone standing across the street under the big tree?"

Turning his head, he looked off across the street. Sure enough, a man stood there. He frowned. A man with black, unkempt hair—much like his own—wore a jeweled sword from his right hip.

"I thought as much." Powell rocked back on his heels. "It's a strange night. Sometimes one of his kind will come by and urge me to move on, but I'm not leaving my home." The old man shook his gray-covered head. "But that one has been studying you since you walked up here."

"His kind?" Lash forced air out of his dry mouth.

"You're looking at a gatekeeper, son. A sentinel against the unholy."

Sentinel against the unholy. Lash was counted among the unholy. Did the man think he meant someone harm? He swallowed. He didn't know much of anything if it didn't belong to Netherworld. Of course, the stranger knew he was condemned. He wouldn't be staring Lash down otherwise. But how did he know? Would the stranger attack him?

Lash returned the look. What would it be like to be in the stranger's shoes? To have what had been denied him? Would Lash, in turn, look upon a lost soul with scorn? "And you, sir? How do you know of gatekeepers?"

"Eh, son. I avoid the lighted path."

The lighted path. The old man had been shown the way to the Afterworld and had avoided the road? Why would anyone deny themselves an eternity of Paradise?

"You look like you could use some advice…"

Lash nodded as his heart beat a fast pace. He glanced across the road to check to see if the man had disappeared. The sentinel still stood watch.

"Trust in our Lord." Without another word, Powell walked right through the door and into the funeral home.

Lash rubbed his eyes, unsure of what he'd just seen or who he'd spoken to. Across the street, the gatekeeper hadn't moved.

A couple exited the building. The man made eye contact before he guided the teary-eyed woman past. A moment later, two women passed him on the way to their auto.

He grabbed the door and opened it when he saw an old woman approaching it. She walked, pushing some piece of equipment along. An elderly man shuffled behind the old woman.

Surprised, he released the door once the couple had cleared it. His hand hadn't been burned and was still attached to his arm. At home in Netherworld, if he'd touched something off-limits, he'd have been punished right away.

He blew out a slow breath. Nothing stopped him from going inside, except for the sentinel who stood across the street. Well, and the fact that the floor could open up. That might be difficult to explain to Teva.

The unknown had him waiting.

He backed up along the building to where he could keep an eye on the gatekeeper. Several more people left the funeral home before Teva exited. "Hey, you."

They fell in step together. "Hey."

"It wasn't so bad."

"Sorry I left you alone."

"Oh, no. Hey, it was fine." Teva clasped his arm as they moved forward. "Jenna's family was nice and polite. Ally had already come and gone."

"Too bad you missed her." While Teva settled inside he slid

into the jeep. "Teva, across the street, what do you think of that tree?"

She stretched her neck up. "Looks pretty old. Why?"

Lash frowned. "Is that all you see there?"

"Yep. Just an old oak tree."

The sentinel still stood underneath the high, wide branches. Teva didn't possess the ability to see the gatekeeper. He'd needed to be sure.

She got the car going and pulled out into the road. Only then did the gatekeeper move. As they passed by, the man walked into the street and folded his arms across his chest.

Lash looked behind them. The sentinel stood with his legs braced wide as cars passed.

"What do you see back there?" Teva adjusted the little mirror over the front window.

Someone who fought against everything unholy. "Nothing." He turned back around. Finally, the legion lords would leave him be...only to have those of the Afterworld appear.

Just my luck.

ᙅ

Lash's appetite for Teva stayed hot in his loins with her nearness. The night had grown deep. Dawn would break across the horizon soon. He enjoyed watching the Earth wake. Teva curled up to his side. Her head kept nodding into his shoulder. She was sleepy and should be in bed, asleep and alone. But instead, she lay resting beside him.

He sighed. "Bedtime."

"Oh, not yet. I'm awake."

He grunted. "Your eyes are little slits."

She gasped. "Do I look that bad?" She pushed to sit upward.

"Not at all." In truth, he wanted to hold her and ease her tiredness. She'd stayed up with him, for him. He required little sleep and watched cartoons to pass time. "Go to bed. And I'll clean up here."

"Oh, no, I'll help."

"Fine. I'll put you to bed." He sat up, then scooped her up into his arms. She squealed while he stood up.

"Oh, gosh. Nic, put me down. I know I'm heavy."

He frowned. She wasn't heavy. Not at all. In Netherworld, he could handle burdens five times his weight. He was a good, dependable slave. She didn't weigh anything near what he did.

After a moment of struggle, she wrapped her arms around his neck. Her breasts flattened against his chest. "Don't drop me."

As if.

He inhaled. He'd never get enough of her unique scent. Surely Paradise didn't smell any better. When he went home, he'd treasure the memory of her scent as much as he would her and her touch.

The soft pant of her breath teased him. His cock hardened, so rigid it ached.

A gentle hand tangled into his hair.

He groaned, finally arriving inside her room. "Here you go." He released her legs, only to have her arms continue to cling to his neck. "Teva..."

"Kiss me, Nic."

His heart thundered in his chest. Beat in his ears. Lust surged to his cock to tighten his balls.

A kiss...

"A kiss goodnight can do neither of us any harm."

Not able to argue, hungrily, he dipped his head. She rose up on tiptoe to press her lips to his. He groaned at the jolt of desire that rushed through his veins. His hands held a steady grip on her hips.

Soft lips brushed across his mouth.

Arousal beat strong within him. His hands drifted up along her back.

She moaned.

Her lips and teeth teased as she writhed in his arms.

His cock twitched. His balls tightened in warning at the promise of release. Licking, she tugged at his mouth until he opened, allowing her to seek entrance. Her tongue dove into his mouth to toy with his own. She tasted of the grapes and cantaloupe they'd snacked on.

Lash growled as hunger beat stronger. His hands drifted down to capture her ass. He cupped her in his palms to press his hard length into her soft belly. Need boiled hot in his balls. He wanted to come, but most of all he wanted Teva. He ached to stuff her with his cock until he exploded into her soft depths.

Teva sucked on his tongue. Arousal intensified until he could barely breathe. Her hands ran across his shoulders and upper arms. The touch scorched him as nails raked a path of fire where ever they touched.

He rocked his hips into the thrust of her grinding belly. Lash moaned. Never had he known such pleasure.

The kiss deepened as he dipped her head back and took control. Now his tongue turned bolder to delve in, to tease hers. Once he'd explored her crevices at his leisure, he sucked her tongue.

Teva panted as she broke the kiss. "Nic..."

His chest heaved. So close to the edge, a simple touch and he'd come in his jeans. "I'm...s..."

"Oh, no." She shook her head. "It was a great goodnight kiss. The best I've ever had." Softly, she placed her lips to his in a feather-light kiss. "Goodnight, Nic. Thank you."

He stepped back.

"I'm sure the alarm will wake you soon."

"That's fine." He stepped further back toward the door. "Goodnight, Teva." Shame heavy on his shoulders, he turned away. He should have had more control.

In the living room, he collected the pizza box from the meal they'd picked up after the viewing. After he tossed the box in the trash, he rinsed out the glasses they'd used and put them inside the sink.

His cock was still thick when he went outside. The screen door closed with a snap.

Desire and shame. What a battle. He shouldn't have kissed Teva, yet he'd been unable to resist. And now, she'd be more tempting than ever.

His hands trembled as he pulled his cock free of the confines of his pants. With rough motions, he stroked himself to climax. On a groan, his come splattered the dry ground.

Heart beating a fast rhythm, he caught his breath. Even with the sexual tension eased, the shame remained. He'd touched something pure.

He'd dirtied Teva with his ungodliness.

His head dropped back. Lord help him, he wanted to touch her again and again. He wanted to do far more then taste her sweet mouth. And given the chance, he might.

Chapter Nine

Teva moved a box out of the way to reach another she sought. She had to be getting close. They were down to slim pickings. Worry knotted her belly. She wouldn't have thrown her mom's book of magic away by accident? Or her mom's craft tools? Would she?

Nic backed out of the closet. "Think I've found it." He extended his arm to hand her a thick journal.

A full sentence. The first one of the day. Nic had never been much of a talker, but he'd been real quiet during the morning. His silence brought guilt up from last night. What a great kiss they'd shared. The moment would remain remarkable to her. Still, she'd taken advantage of his nearness...of him. After all, he'd admitted he was a virgin. He probably didn't kiss too often, since it could lead to sex.

So instead of cleaning her cabins, she'd set about finding her mom's spells. With the journal clasped to her breast, she navigated the boxes to get to the hallway.

Nic followed to the doorway, "You still want these outside?" He pointed to several stacked boxes in the nearest corner.

"That'd be great." They'd discovered a half-dozen cartons containing clothes neither of her parents had worn. At least, not that she could recall. The items would be the first to go.

"Do you need help moving them?" She eyed the boxes. They were some of the largest in the room.

"Not at all."

"Thanks." She drank in his masculine strength. "Okay then, I'm going to get us some lunch going while you finish up here."

He nodded and turned away.

In the kitchen, she placed her mom's book on the table. Next, she set the front screen door to stay open for Nic to get in and out easily.

Effortlessly, she put some red beans on to reheat along with some fresh rice. Red beans and rice couldn't be beat for a quick meal.

Nic walked by with another box braced on his shoulder as she sat down. Her hands trembled as she flipped the cover over. She ran her fingers over the writing. *Spell book of Regina Gibson.*

Oh, Mommy, I miss you.

Now more than ever, she regretted not forcing her mom to share the gift of magic with her. Magic had been so important to her mom, while Teva had loved the land they'd lived on more. And so she'd allowed her mom to close her out of that facet of her life. Her mom had spent hours making spells to share with those in need. And Teva had spent her days with wildlife.

She turned another page and another, through a charming collection of blessings.

Tears burned her eyes as she flipped through some spells. *Fertility. Bring fortune. Bring fame. Sexual attraction.*

Now *that* was a spell she didn't need. Moisture pooled from her sex from the mere thought of the man in the other room, and she shifted in her seat. Nic had been so hot last night.

Love. Soul mate.

Did anyone dare to bind with another forever?

"This your mom's?" Nic held out an envelope. "I found it in the closet."

"Oh, it might be." The letter wasn't sealed. It only had the lip of the envelope tucked inside.

Slowly, with shaking hands, she pulled a letter from inside. Once she unfolded it, she read.

Dearest Teva,

I imagine if you're reading this, I've gone on to the next plane of existence. Though your interest in something that has meant so much to our female ancestors pleases me ...I must ask you to honor your promise.

Do not pursue magic.

Magic was important to me from my first steps. My own mother fine-tuned my skills with loving care. And when you reached high school and lacked the deep involvement necessary to keep control of the power within our grasp...I accepted your will.

Magic isn't for everyone and in some cases should be kept from others. While I trust you to know the difference between right and wrong, I don't feel the same about all of our loved ones.

I'm sure you can recall when I myself lost the true spark for our magic. There's a reason behind the denial of my craft. Your aunt Clarisse—my sister—is now so deep in the black arts, there's no way of saving her. I've tried many times.

Dearest, stay away from her. Clarisse's acceptance of the dark side did more than sadden me.

And remember—if you're ever left without a choice—spell work is best created for yourself. While it's possible to follow a spell written by me or another, it's best to adapt the spell to suit your own purposes.

I hope one day we meet again.

Blessings with love,

Mom

"You all right?" Nic still stood beside her. His voice startled her. She'd been so deep in reading, she'd forgotten he was there.

Mouth dry, she could barely think straight. "Um, Mom says I need to stay away from Clarisse."

"What?" His face tightened.

"Do you want to read it?" She held the letter out to him.

Nic raised a hand. "I cannot read."

"Oh. Are you sure?" She wanted to take the words back, but it was too late. Of course, everyone knew many slipped through the cracks and never learned to read. A person would forget the ability to read about as much as they'd forget a wife. "I'll read it again out loud."

Nic pulled a chair around the table and sat down. His knee brushed her leg. Comfort. Appreciative, she slid to the edge of her seat to get closer to him as she read.

Nic listened silently. Finished, she put the letter back in the envelope.

"Explain this magic she speaks of."

"Oh, Mom... Well, we're from a long line of Celtic Druid priestesses. If you're one with nature, if you believe in your own power..." She'd never attempted to explain magic before. "Mom's spell book contains spells from centuries back. I guess Mom's saying Clarisse has gone bad. She's embraced the dark side of magic." Somehow, Teva could hear James Earl Jones from *Star*

Ware in her head. She shook it off.

Nic didn't even blink.

"I can see how easy it could be to fall into that. I mean magic should never be practiced for personal gain or for one's self. It should always benefit all parties involved. But...black magic practitioners don't have the same..." She shrugged. "...guidelines."

Her lip caught between her teeth. She could remember when Clarisse had changed. It'd been a big change. Her mom had rarely spoken to or of her aunt after that summer...Was Clarisse desperate enough to embrace darkness?

A quiver raced down her spine.

Was her aunt now dangerous? Had there been more to her visit the other day? Lord, she'd invited the woman inside. Did the invitation stand forever now that it had been made?

"Teva?"

She glanced over.

"I think something is burning."

"Oh, damn. Lunch." She dashed into the kitchen, but was too late to save much of the beans.

At the table, Nic tucked the letter back into a crease in the spine and closed her mom's journal. "You should listen to your mom. Magic and power can lead to bad situations."

She sighed.

Getting him to accept her help wasn't going to be easy.

☙

Lash eased his thigh away from Teva. She tended to sit far too close. And while he enjoyed the jolt it never failed to give, it wasn't a good thing. He swallowed. He needed release and wanted nothing more than to pull his hard cock out to jerk off until he erupted. The kiss they'd shared would forever be with him. She'd been so warm. So welcoming. But, in the eyes of the Afterworld, he was a monster.

He couldn't taint her with more of his touch. He wouldn't ruin Teva.

If he could endure any punishment meted out by a legion lord without pleading for mercy, he could control his lust.

"You want to watch a show before we turn in?"

Sweat beaded his palms, and he wiped them on his jeans. An ache pulsed in his cock as it pressed heavily against the fabric. He shook his head. "I didn't like the mother deer dying in that last one."

Her mouth turned down. "Yeah, that was a bummer. I've got one about mer-people you might like."

"Mer-people?"

"You know, people who are part fish and live in water."

He grunted, pretty sure he hadn't met any mer-people in Netherworld. Then again, most often when you were tossed into the underworld ocean, a Megalodon ate you. Repeatedly. Until a lord got bored and dragged you out.

He shuddered. The legion lords had forgotten about him once, and he'd spent a violent year with a Megalodon.

"They're just mythical creatures."

She'd already explained mythical to him. In fact, his ancestors were part of her legends. So, who was to say a race of mer-people didn't exist?

"I've got plenty of football games taped." Her arm brushed his. "Or we can take a walk. You seem to like the outdoors."

A rapid pace kicked up in his heart. She paid attention to

his likes. Nothing compared to the environment—well, maybe anywhere where Teva was. But he liked to breathe fresh air and liked the wide-open sky. It didn't matter if it was day or night. The vile atmosphere of Netherworld haunted him. So he wanted as much of the outdoors as he was allowed.

Yet more quiet time with Teva unnerved him. Watching movies had proved trying enough. He wiped his hands on his jeans again.

"Hey, I promise I won't kiss you again." Her voice sounded so soft, he had trouble hearing her.

He inhaled roughly through his nose as his cock twitched with need.

"Hey, it's okay." She stood up. "I understand. You're saving yourself for Mrs. Right."

"Mrs. Right?" He averted his gaze from her breasts, only a foot from his eyes. Above that, her mouth. She stood too close. He fisted his hands so he wouldn't press his cock against her. Or reach out and touch the tempting peaks of her swollen nipples. It was as if she were naked, he could make out the peaks so clearly through the shirt.

He'd noticed she always dressed different closer to bedtime than she did through the day. Not that her short pants didn't wreak enough havoc on his lust, but the thin tops she wore to bed…

Breasts. Thighs. Her mouth. And her ass had been a perfect fit for his hands last night while they'd kissed.

His balls drew up.

"Oh, you know, your soul mate." When she turned, her curls bounced. "Someone perfect for you."

He closed his eyes. *What to say?* Maybe he read too much into her touches?

Yes. That was it. The lust running through him had taken over his mind. Often it was difficult to think past the arousal. He'd read far too much into her actions. There was no fear of her caring for him.

He stood. "It's late." He looked at the star-filled night. There were no stars in Netherworld.

"Kind of early compared to our last couple of nights." She held her ground.

True. The previous nights had been spent together until she nearly slept in his arms.

"Seriously, no more pressure. You're abstaining. It's cool." She headed over to her jeep and climbed inside for a moment. When she reappeared, she held a light of some sort. "Let's go."

On a sigh, he fell in step beside her. Lash listened to the little creatures talking to one another. Teva's light panned back and forth in front of their path.

They remained silent until they reached the road. While his blood cooled a degree, his cock stayed stiff.

"It is nice out here."

"Yes." He'd stay forever, if allowed.

"My dad and I used to walk out here." She sighed. "Mom hated being outside at night."

"Why?" He frowned. The outdoors soothed him like nothing else.

"Oh, she was deathly afraid of things that go bump in the dark." She walked down the road, and he stayed with her pace. "She hated horror movies, too."

He looked around. There was no evilness around them. Only night with its creatures. If something evil hid out there, he'd sense the danger. He belonged to that world, and the Prince's mark assured he'd never escape its hold. "What are horror movies?" he asked, though he could guess.

"Oh." Teva made a motion to slit her throat. "Blood and gore. Icky stuff, really. They're a big draw for young moviegoers. You know, vampires. Zombies and demons. "

The hairs on his arms stood on end. "Teva?"

"Hmmm?"

"Demons are real. They're not part of a fictional world you've explained to me." He held his breath in wait for the coming punishment.

Nothing happened. Only Teva shifted to walk closer to his side. Her arm rubbed his with each step. "Yeah, well, some cultures believe in them. But..." She laughed nervously. "I think I'm ready to go back and watch a mer-princess enchant a prince."

He turned around as she did. He'd frightened her. Good. Because it was deathly important she accept the reality of demons. They meant her real harm. And, though he'd held out so far, it was only a matter of time before another lost soul or darken went after her spirit.

❦

Teva rolled over on to her back and moaned. What a night. She was hot, inside and out. Nic confused her. After their walk, they'd watched another movie of her collection, one they both enjoyed, and it got rid of the shadow demons. Though she'd tried not to cuddle like before, she'd craved his nearness.

Now she couldn't sleep. Nic had called it a night and had gone to shower. Lord, all she could do was imagine what he was doing in there.

Warm water and soap. There'd been no hiding the erection

he'd been packing most of the night.

Slow, hot sensations of pleasure fluttered to life in her belly and traveled to her sex.

Arousal tingled in her clit. Unable to fight it any longer, she trailed her fingers down her belly to bury in her wet crotch. The cloth of the hipsters she wore constricted her movements. Frustrated, she eased them down to cover her hips, and then kicked them off.

Once her head was comfortable on the pillow again, her fingers got busy. She caught her clit between two fingers and worked the bundle of nerves.

Liquid pooled as pleasure built. Sweat beaded her breasts. Her nipples rubbed the material that hid them.

Teva moaned and eased the friction. She didn't want to come too fast. She spread her legs wide and ran her fingertips up and down her clit. She dipped two fingers into her hole and imagined they were Nic's.

His would be longer. Reach deeper. And have more force with a different angle. She moaned, enjoying the feel of her soft walls clenching her buried digits.

She wanted Nic. But she'd settle for a climax. Her fingers left her hole to clamp around her clit once more. Frantically, she rubbed the swollen flesh between her fingertips. Her hips arched as she panted. Her toes curled as the pleasure intensified.

Her thighs tensed.

An achy need to be filled consumed her, and she thrust her hips up to meet an imaginary lover. Her belly tightened, anticipating the bliss.

Teva's body tensed at the pulsing sensation bursting in her clit to flow outwards. She moaned, flicking her clit until the last of the convulsions passed.

She waited for her heart rate to calm. For her breathing to ease.

On a panting breath, she rolled onto her side. She'd needed the sexual relief of pent-up arousal. Surely she'd be relaxed tomorrow. Less likely to need to jump Nic's bones.

Reaching out, she turned on the little potpourri pot she kept on the bedside table. The light fragrance from the oil would soothe her to sleep as it heated. Fragrance therapy had always been one of her indulgences.

Sheet in her hands, she adjusted her covers as her eyes drifted closed. Sleep would be easy, with Nic to star in her fantasies.

Only Teva wanted out of the fantasy that gripped her. It was no dream, but a nightmare come to life. She looked around in a full-blown panic.

Spiders.

Great big, hairy spiders hunted her, with no escape in sight. And no Nic.

Her feet pounded on the stone floor as she ran.

The click of pincers followed in her wake. Her breath, along with the buzz of the spiders' communication, echoed in the cavern.

Heart beating in her ears, she slid to a stop. Spiders now advanced from in front. With a glance over her shoulder, she saw she couldn't go back.

Click. Click. Click. The pincers snapped a deadly reminder.

Frantically, she scrambled up the side of the rock wall into a tighter cavern. She raced down the dark tunnel.

The spiders followed.

She slipped in something slimy. Rebounded to the click of

pincers.

She screamed when she fell forwards. She landed in what could only be spiders' eggs. *The squeak and hum of communication increased.*

Teva screamed once more, awakening in Nic's arms.

"Shh." He soothed her, holding her close.

"Oh my God." She cried and wrapped her arms around his neck. "Oh my God. I've never had a dream like that." *Not ever.* She'd never been prone to nightmares or even bad dreams. And that had been a nightmare of the worst kind.

Her spider phobia.

"You're okay now." He held her close to his warm, bare body.

Not convinced, she clung to him. The giant spiders still vaguely taunted her from the shadows of her room. "Oh, Nic, I can't believe how real that felt."

"Shh." He rubbed her back with both hands. "I'm here. I came as soon as I heard you call out."

She released a shaky breath. She was being silly over the dream, but it'd been so real. "There were spiders as large as my room chasing me."

"Shh. Don't worry now." His hands continued to massage her back. And oddly, not only his touch, but his presence calmed her.

Composed now, she relaxed in his arms. Her body pressed against the hard planes of his chest. "It was probably that spider you saved the other day, manifested in my dream. That's all."

Nic remained silent. His hands now aroused instead of soothed.

She squirmed closer.

He grunted. The erection extending from his body caught between them.

"I'll let you rest now."

"Don't leave me yet." She tangled her hand in his hair.

Chapter Ten

"I want you, Nic." Teva's need vibrated through his body to settle an ache in his balls. He gulped air. He had to get out of the room. Away from her. Only, her clinging arms held him in place. She needed him. His comfort. His touch.

He didn't want to taint her. But it'd been so long since he'd been touched for anything other than to cause him pain or shame.

A shudder of desire racked his body. Pleasure engulfed him. He tightened his arms around her soft body. "Shh." His hand got caught up in her curls as he cupped the back of her head.

The curve of her bare hip pressed into his thick cock.

She squirmed.

Lash moaned. *Give me strength.*

He needed to push her away. Now, before it was too late. Breath ragged, he eased her body from his. His hands clasped to her upper arms, he jerked at the feel of her hand on his cock.

"You want me, too." Her grip tightened as her palm slid upward along his rigid length, then back down to the base. "I know you do."

How I want you. A rough breath burst from his nostrils.

Come on. Lie to her.

Firm fingers stroked his cock.

Teva, you're so beautiful. His chest tightened. What to say? Need and want warred with what was right. He had to do it. "I don't want this."

Her hand stilled but didn't leave his cock.

"Not now." Lash's teeth clenched together as he tried to keep control, not an easy task with her hand resting on him.

No punishment struck him for the lie.

Her grip loosened to allow him to stand up. Regret at the loss of her touch clutched at his chest.

Quickly, she pulled the sheet up to hide her naked lower half. "Um, I'm sorry about that." A shaky hand went through her curls. "I don't know what came over me."

Don't be sorry.

"Don't worry about it." He clenched his fists to keep from taking her in his arms again. He'd hurt her. Something he'd sought to avoid above all things. "Goodnight, Teva. I'll see you in the morning."

She rolled away from him. "'Night."

In his room, he put his jeans on. He'd start sleeping in them. After a quick check to see if Teva was still in bed, he went outside to sit on the porch.

In all the time he'd spent in Netherworld, he'd never been so tested. Punishments couldn't control him. Not once had he turned on another lost soul. Not once had he raised his fists to a darken. And the darkens were the worst with their continuous goading.

But Teva? His need for her, he couldn't control. His lust burned hotter with each passing day. All he wanted to experience was her touch. He wanted the memory of claiming her to keep with him to Netherworld. What would it feel like to be taken without condition, without strings attached, into her body? He wanted everything Teva would willingly give him.

What a monster you are, for wanting such impossible things.

Outside, Lash inhaled the night air. His touch would lead her to an eternity of darkness. He'd delve deeper within to locate the strength he needed to resist the greatest temptation of his lives.

Abruptly, the air shifted before him, and he stood in expectation of the worst. Only it wasn't a legion lord who appeared.

A glowing woman floated before his eyes. He blinked. She remained there.

"Hello." She flipped her long red hair over her shoulder. She looked vaguely familiar.

A frown creased his brow as he studied the vision.

"Hello." She waved a hand before his face. "Can you see me?"

He nodded.

"I thought so." She glanced around. "I don't have much time or nearly enough power to stay long."

Lash stared, with no clue what she talked about. Never had he seen anything like her before. Her kind didn't exist in Netherworld. She was far too bright.

"I'm Teva's mother."

Ah. He *had* seen her, then. She'd been in the pictures of all the roller coasters. "What are you?"

"A saved soul."

If only he could share that news with Teva.

"I've come to ask you a favor." The light that surrounded her dulled when her feet finally touched the Earth.

A favor. His heart pounded with dread. He had no wish to be placed directly between good and evil.

"I'd like for you to make me a promise."

Lash sat back down. Between good and evil, he'd struggle for Teva. After all, he couldn't imagine any punishments he hadn't already suffered. "What is it?"

"I want you to go back to where you've come from."

He closed his eyes. That wasn't something he wanted to do or even could do. In fact, he didn't know for sure how to get home without the help of a legion lord, and as far as he could tell, after the Prince's visit he'd been left on his own, at least for the time being.

"If you cannot, I want you to call forth your guardian."

A rough sound forced its way from his chest. *He had no guardian.*

"Teva won't believe their existence, but you will. Everyone on the Earth plane has a guardian. Including you." Her hand fluttered. "I'm revealing far too much as it is. I cannot call forth a guardian myself."

"How?" Though he didn't buy a guardian offering him any help, for Teva, he needed to know how to summon one.

"I fear for my daughter. If things get bad for her...for you...pray to the Lord. Say you need intervention, and if the fates will it, yours will arrive. You may be able to see him, since you're condemned. Normally, they're invisible to the human eye."

So the woman knew he was among the damned. And still she asked for his assistance. It was rumored that a mother would do anything for her child. Now he had the evidence of it.

"I must return home." The woman tilted her head and hovered above the ground. "I dare not intervene any further."

Her glow intensified before she disappeared. "I beg you" echoed across the warm wind.

He glanced around the clearing from Teva's porch. He was alone. He half expected a darken or lord to appear after the visit from the saved soul. But his feelers picked up nothing from the dark world.

An ache slowly beat in the back of his skull. It was a different kind of pain than he'd suffered before.

A guardian for a lost soul?

It sounded like a tale a legion lord would spread to get a lost soul to grieve themselves into despair with their hopes of finding one. He was no fool. Yet, why would Teva's mom appear to ask him to do this, if it was anything less than true?

༼༽

The alarm jarred her awake. She reached out and hit the snooze button. She hated mornings. Hated getting up early. Most days, she would like nothing better than to sleep in. Right now, she at least had a morning perk. She pulled the covers up around her for warmth.

Nic.

He'd already be up. Probably outside.

Last night flooded back to her in a rush. "Oh, crap." She scrambled up. After he'd left her room, she'd reset her alarm for an hour earlier in hopes of missing him. She needed some time alone to think herself into misery.

She'd been a slut last night, throwing herself at him that way.

Covering her face, she groaned. What must he think of her now? Was there hope he didn't think she simply wanted to score with a virgin? Everyone knew it was a common occurrence for a guy to want...Would he turn the tables and think that of her?

Teva sighed.

The guy probably wanted some time alone, too. To rethink her generosity. Disgusted with herself, she tossed the pillow aside. Quickly, she put on clean panties and slid into some khaki shorts, a bra and a tank top.

In the bathroom, she got ready to face the day. With a glance in the mirror, she applied lip gloss.

Back in her room, she grabbed socks and her short boots. Beside the bed, she plopped down. God, it was early. Far too early for anyone normal to be up.

She leaned over and inhaled the now-cool, fragrant oil. She sighed. The sensuous scent had always appealed to her, but she hadn't forgotten the nightmare yet. A chill stood the fine hair on her forearms on end. Coward that she was, she associated the scent with the dreams. She'd try another fragrance tonight. She made a mental note to change the oil.

Shoes on, she crept past Nic's room. A peek inside showed his bed was already made. At the sight, her feet slowed. So much for avoiding him for a while.

The front screen door closed softy behind her. Nic knelt on his haunches on the porch. "Good morning, Teva."

"Hey." The heat rushed to her neck and face. "I thought you might still be sleeping."

"I didn't expect you up so soon. The alarm only sounded once." The right side of his mouth lifted in a smile.

Pleasure swamped her body to curl her toes. *Holy moly, he'd teased her.* The embarrassment from last night faded.

"Well, we're both up." She folded her arms to try and hide

her puckered nipples.

"And early, too." The gentle smile was back in place as he stood.

An urge to kiss him nearly had Teva throwing herself at him. She caught her lip between her teeth. "Oh stop, will you?"

"I have the impression you were trying to slip off alone."

Oh...

"Um, not really." At least, not any longer. She scuffed a foot across the wood plank she stood on.

Nic looked away, and she was thankful he didn't push. He turned back to meet her gaze. "Did you have any more bad dreams?"

A tremor raced up her spine. "Yeah, it was an odd night. I've never been much of a dreamer, much less prone to nightmares."

Nic nodded once. "You need me, you call for me. Anytime. Day or night." His lashes lowered to hide his black eyes. "Teva?"

"What?"

"You ever want me gone from here, just say the word."

She sucked in a breath.

"I appreciate your kindness, but I don't want to make you uncomfortable in any way." He shoved his hands into his back pockets. "I mean it, Teva. I'll go. No problems whatsoever."

"Hey." Panic thumped in her chest. She'd made him uncomfortable. Really uncomfortable. God, the guy didn't have anywhere to go, and he was willing to leave. All because she couldn't keep her hands to herself. *Great going, Teva.* "About last night..."

"No." He shook his head. "Don't worry about last night. I'm talking about me. I think I may be bad luck. Jenna's death, your aunt showing up, and now your bad dreams." He looked around, as if expecting something else to happen from him talking about it.

She gasped. *Him? Bad luck?* The poor guy. More guilt than ever weighed on her shoulders. She would keep a better rein on her hormones around him. How could she have forgotten the trauma he'd been through? *Geez, Teva, the guy can't even remember his last name.* "Oh, Nic, look, you are not bad luck."

He looked about to say something, but stopped.

"Hey, I mean it. You're not bad luck." She clasped his muscular arm and a spark of arousal stirred to quicken her breath. His black gaze held her captive. "Nic, it's been great having you here. I mean it. Please don't think that way."

He nodded.

Taking a step back, she folded her arms across her breasts. This sealed it. She would delve into her mom's magic and find the right spell to help Nic. "How about I make some French toast for breakfast, and we can head out to the cabins. I have two new arrivals this afternoon."

"You sure you don't want to take a nap?" The tiniest of smiles gentled his face. "It's still early. I can work by myself for a while."

"Oh, stop." She rolled her eyes. "I'm fine now. It's just waking up that I'm slow at."

ಬ

Lash looked from the television screen to Teva. She sat crossed-legged near the table, which took up a lot of the living room. "Are you sleepy?" She'd yawned many times since she'd pushed play to start the movie.

It had been a long day. Though none of the work had been

tedious or torturous, Teva had gotten tired. A late-arriving camper had kept them away from her home later than usual. Upon their return, there'd been no stopping her from reading her mom's journal.

"Nope. Not at all."

He frowned at the clear lie.

"So, what do you think of the show?" A smile spread across her pretty mouth.

He munched some popcorn. He'd committed a sin tonight. Besides his lustful fantasies about Teva, he'd eaten three bags of popcorn all by himself. A clear glutton.

"It's fine." They now watched what was known as a "chick flick". The giggling store clerk had chatted on and on about how cool he was to suffer through a girl's movie. Teva had picked several films in the genre.

If the girl or Teva ever knew what true suffering entailed, it would blow their minds.

"You sure you don't mind watching it?" Her nose curled.

"I don't mind." He minded having his balls sliced off. He minded being tossed into a pit of quicksand or lions. *Kate and Leopold* wasn't a bother.

She placed the leather strap she was weaving down on the table. "We could listen to some music instead?"

"No, thank you." He let a smile grow. He didn't like her music and got enough of it in the auto as they traveled. It was too loud for him. He preferred peace and quiet. Netherworld had abused his ears enough with all the crying and suffering echoed in its depths.

"Let me get you some more popcorn."

"Wait." But she was already up and moving toward the kitchen. He sighed. Now he'd have to eat more. He'd never be wasteful, having seen too much waste already in Netherworld.

In the kitchen, Teva worked, and he focused on the show once more. People led different lives from the roles they acted. Actors could have many lovers in their movies. The subject was as interesting as it was confusing. He couldn't figure out how the actors didn't develop real affections for one another. Cartoon characters had it much easier.

"I brought you some more to drink, too." Teva placed another bottle of water along with another bag of popcorn on the table within his reach.

"Thank you."

"Anytime." She smiled and sat back down to her work. "I'm going to make you a good-luck charm."

Lash stared. They'd already discussed this on the way back to her home. The woman was far too stubborn. "I'm not the one who needs good luck or protecting." Changing positions, he sat up straight. He braced his elbows on his knees. "Teva, it's *you* who needs it." There. He'd said it straight out. Maybe now she'd get his meaning since his hint earlier hadn't helped.

A breath rushed from his lungs when nothing happened to him. Still, fear of being tortured in front of Teva kept him on edge. Apparently, unlike that of his hordes, the Prince's word meant something. He'd been left alone. For how long, he couldn't begin to guess.

She snorted. "And, as I said earlier, I'm not the one with a missing memory."

His teeth clenched. His memory was fine.

"That reminds me. How is your back?"

"Fine."

"Nic..." She shook her head. "You say everything is fine. Have you been taking care of it?"

"Yes."

"Great."

They shared a moment of silence. The movie no longer interested him. Only Teva captured his attention.

"My mom wrote a lot on charms centered on Celtic knots." She folded her arms along the journal. "There's a lot about dragons in here, too. What do you think about dragons? I've always been fascinated by the mystical beings."

He tried not to think about dragons. Demon dragons normally ate a lost soul after they'd burned them alive, only to start the torture over once more. Nope, he didn't think a lot about dragons.

"I've run across several crosses made into charms. I'm sure you know about a cross. And all it represents."

The times he'd been crucified were countless. Netherworld had a field dedicated specifically for the purpose of crucifying lost souls who failed to follow a demon lord's order, normally against another lost soul. He nodded. He knew enough. The legion lords took special glee in that field.

"Did you know it's a myth Eve took a four-leaf clover from Paradise when she was expelled?"

He shook his head. He knew little of myths of sacred objects.

"The Irish say it's the first defense against black magic."

With an increased heart rate, he settled back to slouch on the couch.

"Celtic dominance at one time extended across Ireland. It was the Druids or Celtic priests who elevated four-leaf clovers to the status of Celtic charms." Teva lifted her blue eyes. "Allegedly, they're potent against malevolent spirits."

Lash grunted. Now, malevolent spirits, he needed no more

lessons on. They'd taunted him enough.

"The leaves of four-leaf clovers are said to stand for faith, hope, and luck." A blush spread across her cheeks. "And love. I'm going to keep reading Mom's journal, but I think the four-leaf clover is promising." She rubbed a wooden ornament between her fingertips. "Mom even left a crafted charm behind in her tool chest."

"Teva..."

She sighed.

"I think you should be the one to keep your mom's treasure." He left the couch to sit near her on the floor. "You keep it." Desperately, he sought a way to explain the importance of her keeping the charm. He swallowed. "Teva, you know how I appeared?"

She shifted to bring her breast within an inch of his arm. The temptation of her closeness heated his blood. He pushed the desire down. Now was not the time for distraction.

"I just appeared. I can't recall how. Well, what if I just disappear without a word when I leave?"

"You wouldn't leave without a goodbye." Panic clouded her gaze. "Oh, Nic, if this is about last night..."

He pressed his fingertips to her lips, only to remove them, unable to handle the arousal that rushed through his body. His cock swelled to fill out his jeans. "No, no. Not purposely." He'd never hurt her that way, but he had no control of his stay here on Earth. A demon could pull him back home at any time, once the Prince accepted the fact Lash wouldn't hurt Teva. He forced the issue with her. "What if Jenna was right? What if I'm cursed?"

"Nic, don't say that." She took his hand in hers. "You are not cursed. The thought is so wrong. Look. See, this is why you need the charm."

How did he explain to her, without saying he was condemned and committed a great sin by being with her? He would disgust her. And if she learned the truth, that he lived among the damned...she'd turn away from him not only in revulsion, but fear. He wouldn't see that happen. Somehow, he'd avoid the pain.

In a rush, she turned away to fiddle with the leather string she'd been weaving. After another minute, she turned back. "Lean over." The wooden ornament now dangled from the end of the strap.

What a stubborn woman.

Left without a choice, he dipped his head.

Teva moved closer and eased the leather over his head. He straightened to have the four-leaf charm fall against his chest.

She smiled. "It's a nice piece. It's been a long time since I've woven anything. Nice to know I can still do that." Nervously, she eyed the charm. "Do you think it's 'guy' enough to wear? I mean, you can put it in your pocket if you like. It doesn't have to be around your neck."

He didn't understand this talk of 'guy' business. He remembered the store clerk had mentioned that, too. He was as male as the next man. He had a cock to prove it.

With a trembling hand, she picked it up as if to remove it from around his neck. He stopped her by catching her hand in his. "Thank you, Teva. It's guy enough." A slow grin tugged at his mouth. Smiling wasn't something he was used to, but the joy Teva gave him was something he *could* get used to. He'd sorely miss her when he left. Reluctantly, he released her hand.

"Great." The pulse in her throat quickened. "Has anyone ever told you, you have the best smile?"

Lash shook his head.

"Well, you do." A blush climbed her neck to brighten her cheeks. "I'm not flirting or anything. Just stating a fact."

He nodded and sat back as she scooted away. Curvy thighs filled his view as she stood. He swallowed. Need tightened in his balls. He wanted to caress those thighs, to pull her back to the floor.

"My dad carved the four-leaf clover. It's got his initials on it." She leaned over, her breasts swaying as she closed her mom's spell book. "My dad was a neat guy. A true Irishman. He accepted my mom's magic."

He hadn't known his own father well, nor the relationship his parents had shared.

"Well, I guess I'll turn in so I don't have to use my snooze button in the morning." She smiled. "'Night, Nic."

"Goodnight." He enjoyed the bounce of her ass until she disappeared down the hall. He laid his head back on the couch.

An ache in his chest replaced the need of sexual release. A low moan rumbled from deep in his throat.

The most severe punishment in all Netherworld was the fact lost souls retained their hearts.

Chapter Eleven

In the bathroom, Teva took a quick soak. After drying off, she put on a clean pair of panties and t-shirt for bed. Noting the hour, she popped a Who CD into the player and turned the volume as low as possible. The Who was one of her all-time faves. No one had ever matched their unique sound.

After another song, she opened her eyes. It wasn't working. Oftentimes, she preferred to sleep with music, which was a habit from her teens. It used to make her dad crazy.

Out of bed, she switched the WHO to Led Zeppelin. No one beat Robert Plant's voice. "Stairway to Heaven" drifted out, with its eerie sound.

Plopped on the mattress, she opened the nightstand's little drawer and pulled out the oil. She added a drop of fragrance to what remained in the potpourri bowl and turned it on to heat. Securing the cap, she frowned. She replaced the oil and examined the other bottles more carefully. Weird, but she'd only tried three of the five new fragrances she'd purchased online, and now all the seals had been broken.

She sighed and lay back down. She was being silly. With Nic here, things had gotten busy. Maybe she'd forgotten what she had opened.

In the living room, she could hear Nic was still up. He'd taken the movie out and now watched a cartoon. Rolling onto her side, she scrunched her thighs as pleasure hummed in her sex. No more could she deny her dilemma. She was attracted to a stranger.

Not once had she met anyone like Nic. He was so gentle, soft-spoken, big, and downright yummy. Had he ever lost his temper? She doubted it.

Earlier, he'd patched a leak on one of the cabins, and she'd worried about him up there. All day long, she'd fought the urge to wipe the sweat from his forehead.

What would it be like to have a guy like him make love to her? A sigh rushed through her nose.

The sensuous fragrance soothed her. The familiar music lulled her to sleep.

Teva jolted. She was no longer in her bed. The air turned her stomach. After a blink, she tried to focus. It was difficult to see in the near darkness.

Red eyes stared at her. The ground trembled, or her knees shook as the fiery eyes advanced. She backed up until she hit a jagged, cold wall.

An unbearable urge to pee hit her bladder.

God, where am I?

Grasping the wall, she noted the stone texture. A single pair of eyes emerged from the shadows. Teva's head swam. A fat-bellied man with a dragon's tail and serpents for legs slid closer. A whip dangled from his left hand.

Wildly, she shook her head. What was going on? She scrambled along the wall.

Wake up. Wake up. Wake up.

Another creature followed the first. This one had seven snake heads, twice as many faces, and several sets of insects' wings sprouting from its back.

Dear God...

They were followed by a winged man, who had the head of a goat.

Frantic, she moved along the wall to escape. Mouth dried out, she couldn't breathe. Her heart thumped in her ears.

At the turn of her head, her heart stalled, only to kick-start once more.

Dear God...

Other creatures approached from the opposite direction. She'd stepped into a horror movie or nightmares come to life. Teva screamed.

And woke with Nic's arms around her. "Shh...Teva. You're fine now."

The trembling wouldn't stop. The sweat that coated her body chilled. She'd never been so terrified before. With a whimper, she clung to his neck.

"Was it the spiders again?"

A hysterical laugh burst out. "I wish."

"It's okay." He rubbed her back and arms. "You're all right now."

She didn't feel all right. The urge to pee still pressed from the fear. Never one to watch horror movies, she hadn't been prepared for the nightmare, though she was sure horror buffs wouldn't have cared for a real fright. How did Stephen King cope?

"I'm here now." Nic massaged with his big hands, warming her up. "What did you see?"

"Um." Not ready to let go, she clung to his neck. "I saw evil red eyes."

His hands stilled for the briefest of moments. "I've got you now."

"God, I saw things. One had a goat head. Another...had snake legs." She gulped air and closed her eyes. The sensual fragrance engulfed the room now.

"Don't be afraid of the dream. It can't hurt you."

Drowsy after the adrenaline rush, she rested her head on Nic's shoulder. He continued to rub her back from her shoulders to her butt. His hands ran across her hips and back up to her neck. He soothed with his gentle touch.

She wasn't afraid now, but the dream had frightened her terribly. Folklore told if you fell or died in a dream before you woke, you died in your sleep.

Death wasn't something she was ready to accept.

Nic shifted and lay down beside her. Pillowed on his arm, she drifted back to sleep.

03

A sweet ache pulsed in Teva's clit. Her breasts pressed into the hard plane of Nic's chest. She stretched out to leave sleep more fully.

Nic lay on his side facing her. She still used his arm as a pillow. Outside, it was still dark. She dared not roll over to see what time the clock said. This was far too cozy.

Nic in her bed.

After inhaling his masculine scent, she sighed. God, he smelled good.

Seduce him...

Teva closed her eyes. She could right now. Seduce him. When he woke, he'd be in a sleepy state. A weak moment.

There was no denying he wanted her. She'd experienced it too many times already with his looks. She'd lost count of how often she'd caught his dark eyes on her, only to have him look away. The occasional press of his hard body against hers. The contact couldn't all be accidental, since she went out of her way to touch him. He was just shy about sex.

Coax him...

Use those breasts he so enjoys looking at, to coax him into what you want.

Moisture pooled from her sex.

How she wanted to coax him to pleasure. Her nipples puckered to push against the thin material that hid them.

Lure him with soft whispers.

She cuddled slower and brought her mouth to his throat. "Nic, I want you."

Be bold...

"I want you to fuck me." Her lips placed a soft kiss on his warm skin. Liquid heat rushed to her sex.

Be bolder...

"Fuck me hard and fast." Teva sucked in a breath of hot fragrance. She was burning up. She wanted Nic to fill her.

He moaned in his sleep.

That's it. Tease him...

She ran her hand up under the t-shirt he wore, tracing his muscles. Her nails raked his nipple. His hips rolled forward. A whimper escaped her trembling lips. No one had ever awakened her sexuality like Nic.

In the hopes of calming, she inhaled sharply. The sensual scent only enticed her aroused state. A delicious ache hit her clit.

She moaned. She wanted to come. She wanted to come at Nic's touch.

Stimulate him into taking what you offer.

Her nails raked his nipple once more. Sweet sensation tangled low in her belly.

Tempt him...

Panting, Teva slowly slid her hand down to Nic's cock. The long and thick package swelled harder at her massage.

Good girl, ensnare him...

With the heel of her palm, she rubbed along his length.

"Teva," Nic murmured.

She gasped, sucking in the heavy scented air. Teva's palm ran back and forth along his rigid cock. She wanted nothing more than to flick her own clit until she burst in rapture.

"Stop or I'll come." Nic's voice now sounded more alert.

She whimpered. She didn't want to stop. Wanted him to come as much as she wanted to climax.

Quickly, she shifted her hand position to run her fingers along his erection. This time trying to grip him in a caress.

That's it, get him to come. Then he'll be yours...

Yes. She wanted that. For Nic to belong to her. With more pressure, she ran her hand up and down the length of his cock.

Nic groaned. He caught her hand.

Teva cried out at the loss and soon moaned at the feel of the bed beneath her back, and Nic covering her body.

Yes. Now, if she could only get his clothes off.

"Teva."

Almost violently, Teva tangled a hand in his hair and lifted her head to kiss him.

A shudder racked his big body.

She trembled in response as his mouth opened for her entrance. His mouth was warm, his tongue gentle as it played with hers.

She sighed and loosened her grip in his hair. Her hips rocked up in need. She moaned. She wanted to be filled down below the way his tongue now filled her mouth.

The rigid thrust of his cock brought forth a whimper. At this angle, he wasn't hitting the right spot. Frantic, her hands scrambled down his back to pull his shirt up, so she could caress his warm skin.

Hunger and need blurred her mind, until Nic pulled his mouth away. "We must stop." His breath was as uneven as hers. "I...I must stop."

Push him...

She stilled.

Dear God, that hadn't been her own voice.

Push him. You can ensnare him. He's on edge...

She quivered. That clearly hadn't been her voice inside her own head. What was happening to her?

"Teva?" Nic eased to his side to rest on an elbow.

A glance around the darkened room told her they were alone. At least, she didn't see any red eyes.

"What is it? Did I hurt you?"

"You didn't hurt me." She ignored the dull, unfulfilled ache between her legs. He hadn't hurt her. Hadn't made a move on her until she'd come on to him. God, the guy had been asleep. What was happening to her? Last night, she'd played with herself and now this.

"If you don't tell me what it is, I can't help you." He ran his knuckles along her upper arm. "Let me help you."

She rolled away to stare at the tiny glow of the potpourri pot. Using shaky fingers, she turned the pot off. "I don't know what came over me." Ashamed, she curled up into a ball. "I'm

~~sorry about that."~~

"Teva, about what happened. I didn't stop because I don't want you." His voice grew rough. "I stopped because I do." The bed shifted as he left her alone.

☙

The next morning, Teva didn't want to get out of bed. She hit her snooze six times before finally turning the alarm off. She hadn't slept well at all. So she rolled over and went back to sleep. Her bladder forced her from sleep just before noon.

Noon.

Crap. Quickly, she got ready for the day, only to find Nic gone. A soup simmered in the crock pot. The spicy aroma tickled her hunger. The guy was not only a quick learner, he was good.

Outside, her jeep still sat in the driveway, but she couldn't locate Nic. Shielding her eyes, she looked out over the horizon. No one was in sight. The guy must have walked to the cabins. Or he'd left. Her heart constricted.

No. He'd have said goodbye. Even after her shameful act last night, he'd have said goodbye.

Need for her keys drove her back inside. The mail caught her attention as she reached for the keychain. A small package was addressed to her. Nic must have checked it before he left. Odd, besides junk mail and the occasional rental deposit, she never got anything but bills. She opened it to discover a bracelet and note. The note read.

Teva, please accept this blessed offering with all my love.
Clarisse.

A frown turned down her mouth. Clarisse had sent her a gift? Blessed? Really odd. When was the last time she'd gotten anything from her aunt?

Her sixteenth birthday, and her mom had thrown the gift away. Now she couldn't even recall what it'd been. Only that her mom had tossed it right in the trash. They'd never spoken of it afterwards.

Her fingers traced the fine detail of the jewelry. It was a pretty piece, decorated with several gems of her birthstone.

Teva sighed, unsure if she should keep it or not. The clock chimed. Well, that settled her mind. She was in a hurry now. She'd decide later. Without giving it another thought, she placed the blessing into her pocket.

In the jeep, Pink Floyd kept her company on the radio until she reached the lane the cabins sat on. Nic wasn't hard to locate, since they'd talked about what needed to be done today.

He walked out of cabin nine as she cut the engine. Teva licked her lips. He looked hot and sweaty. Liquid heat rushed from her sex. She moaned. *Stop it already.*

Once she climbed out, she slammed the door. He met her at the bumper. "Catch up on your sleep?" A grin teased at his mouth.

Oh boy...

"Why yes, thank you. I did." And just like that, last night seemed to be forgiven, if not forgotten. What a neat guy he was. Or he was a sadist who liked to have women tease him mercurially. "Did you get any sleep?"

"Yes."

"How's it going?"

"I'm finished up here." He shrugged broad shoulders. "The

campers in cabin two had an emergency back home and had to leave early."

"Oh, that's too bad. I'll reimburse what's owed them, then." She was glad Nic was getting comfortable with the business. There was no helping her growing attachment to him.

The breeze caught Nic's black hair and sent it across his face. It didn't seem to bother him. Teva's fingers itched to shove it out of the way. "I thought I'd finish cutting that tree..." He folded his muscular arms.

"Oh, I don't know.'

"There's nothing to worry about now. I even packed a lunch. We can share it."

"I know, but still."

"All I need you to do is show me how to operate the four-wheeler that hauls the woodcart." He looked bound and determined.

"Okay, but I'll go a step further." She tossed him the jeep keys, and he caught them.

"You sure?"

More than sure, she climbed into the passenger side. From day one, she'd noticed he always paid attention. To what she said. To her actions. He didn't have to ask about starting the jeep or getting it into reverse. She helped him move the seat back to give him legroom. He braced his right hand on her seat, looked behind him and pulled out of the little dirt driveway.

Oh yeah, she was more than sure. On the lane, he put it into drive. And though he was slow at first, he never left the lane. He even remembered where the hiking trail was. He parked carefully near the tool shack.

When they stepped out of the jeep, he tried to hand the keys to her, but she stopped him. "You can practice on the way home, too." She showed him on the key ring which key started the four-wheeler. Nic set the lunchbox on the cart before he stacked the wood already cut in the corner pile.

Absently, she rubbed the offering from her aunt. "Hey, guess what I got in the mail?"

"What?" He lifted his head. His black hair once again obscured his eyes.

"A blessed bracelet from Clarisse."

"That so?"

"Yeah."

"A blessing?"

"Yeah."

"How does that make you feel?" He walked to her side.

"I don't know. I guess that's why I brought it up." In truth, she wished her mom was there to tell her what to do about it. "I'm half-tempted to send it back."

"Give it to me." He held out his hand.

Unsure, she held back.

"You wanted to know what I thought, right?"

She nodded.

"Give it to me."

Lower lip caught between her teeth, she handed it over.

Nic dropped it on the ground and stomped on it twice. Then, he bent down and collected the pieces. "Here." He placed the shattered jewelry into her shaky hand. "Now send it back, and tell her what I did to her *blessing*." His lip curled.

She gasped and closed her fist. So much for Nic not having a temper.

Chapter Twelve

The warm water ran down Lash's body as his hand pumped his cock to release. An image of Teva stayed with him, until the last drop of come left his balls and jetted out.

The night had been a rough one with little sleep. Sexual arousal and Teva's dream had kept him awake. Her dreams needed to be stopped. He was half-tempted to call for a guardian, if only he could wrap his mind around the possibility one would offer assistance.

Twisting the knobs, he turned the water off.

When his breathing finally eased, he heard a loud banging at the front door. A persistent one. Quickly, he dried his lower half in a hurry to get the door. He wanted Teva to make up for the sleep she'd lost due to the bad dreams. Besides, she didn't like getting up early.

Dressed in his jeans, he toweled his hair once before hanging the towel up.

He opened the front door to be greeted by an old man with thick gray hair. "Hello there. I'm Jackson." A smile grew between all the hairs on his face. "Officer Jackson. Well, I'm retired."

Lash opened the screen door for the man. "Hello, there. I'm Nic. Lash. Come in. I'll wake Teva."

"No need to do that. Came out here about you, anyway."

He nodded and waved the officer to the kitchen table. "Want a drink?" he asked, remembering Teva had offered her aunt one.

"Coffee would do just fine."

"There's some instant." Lash didn't care for the brew. He preferred water. But Teva said it perked her right up. She'd said first time she'd had the strong drink, she'd still been drinking out of a bottle.

"That'd be fine." The man ran his palm along the table where he sat.

At the counter, Lash put a mug of water to boil in the microwave and poured himself a glass of water. He drank it while he waited. Once the timer chimed, he carried the mug along with the jar of coffee to the table. "Here you go." He went back for a spoon and passed it to Jackson.

"Thanks a bunch." Lash eyed the man as Jackson dumped two healthy spoonfuls into the water. And then he pulled a thin canister from his pocket to add a splash of clear liquid. "Helps my arthritis."

The man took his time stirring.

Lash sat down across from him.

"Well, now, Mr. Lash, I gotta tell you. I can't find a scrap of evidence anywhere of your existence. It's an interesting puzzle." He sipped his drink. "For this old man."

Lash nodded.

"Regina brought me your picture and fingerprints." The man shook his head. "I'm tapped out on resources."

Regina? Teva's mother? Had the man seen a saved soul, too? Could the man tell he was among the condemned? "You mean Teva?" He checked to be sure.

"I go way back with her father. I've never been real good with names." Jackson tapped his head. "And age ain't helping."

A grin curled Lash's mouth. He didn't know a thing about age. He'd died young.

"So I thought I'd stop by and see how you and Teva were getting along." The man's nose twitched. "Meet you myself."

"We're fine."

"You staying here in the house, then?" Jackson inhaled sharply before he picked his mug up for another drink.

"Yes." No shame lowered his lashes. Well, maybe only a little. Teva was pure, while he was damned. He supposed there was something wrong in those facts alone. But he hadn't defiled Teva with his touch.

"I thought you might be staying in one of the cabins. I hear tell you're working for her now." Jackson sipped the brew.

He frowned. In his time, neighbors took passing people in. When Teva had accepted him into her home so readily, he'd guessed the people on Earth hadn't changed all that much. "I'm helping her where I can."

"That's good. Never thought it right, her being all alone out here."

A chill stood the hairs on the back of his neck on end. He didn't like to think of Teva way out here all alone once he descended back to Netherworld. And what if the Prince sent another after Teva? His fists clenched, and he brought them into his lap to hide them from the old man's scrutiny.

Moisture clung to several of the old man's facial hairs. "Teva sent me an e-mail asking about getting you some identification." Jackson shook his head. "I still can't get used to e-mail."

Unsure what the man spoke of, Lash nodded as if he

understood. Identification he knew of. Teva had been asked for identification at the grocery store. It had her picture. But he couldn't recall if Teva had mentioned e-mail or not. But mail, he checked for her when she slept late. A driver brought it nearly every day in a small rolling box.

"Don't talk much, do you?"

"I suppose not."

Jackson finished his coffee with a sigh. "Nothing wrong with being quiet. Anyway, you and Teva come see me when you're ready for that identification. I'll pull some strings."

Lash nearly told the man there'd be no need. But Jackson was harmless and a good resource for Teva. He didn't want to jeopardize that.

The old man lumbered to his feet. "Thanks again for the coffee."

"You're welcome."

At the door, the old man's nose twitched once more. "You smell anything peculiar?"

He sniffed. "Only the lingering scent of Teva's lamp oil."

Jackson grunted. "Women. Tell Regina to call me if she needs anything."

It was on the tip of his tongue to correct the old man, but instead, Lash moved to show the man out. "I will."

The old man pulled open the door. "Memory's a little slow to take off, but my sniffer is right on the mark. I wish I could place that smell. It's going to make me crazy until it comes to me. "

Jackson amused Lash, considering the sense of smell was a big part of memory. He hadn't given the fact much thought. He could recall the scent of his mother's bread. And he was particularly fond of the way Teva's hair smelled. Still it was hard to figure how Jackson would recall the scent if he couldn't even remember Teva's name, though she did have her mom's eyes.

"You have a good day, you hear?" The outer door squeaked as it was pushed forward.

"You, too." Lash shut the front door once he'd watched the man drive away.

Wandering down the hallway, he braced a shoulder on Teva's bedroom doorframe. She still slept. What would it be like to be allowed to crawl back in bed and hold her close? He inhaled noisily at the familiar stir of arousal. His cock swelled from semi-erect to hard.

The cover had been kicked away. He appreciated the little pants she wore to bed. They were so small they barely covered her rounded ass. On her stomach, her leg was hiked up so her knee rested near her breast. A clear impression of her pussy showed through the thin cloth.

He licked his lips. He wanted to taste her more than anything else.

Then, he wanted to fuck her.

He pushed away from the door. At her bedside, he covered her back up. Teva wasn't for him. He had stop to being a lustful dog.

෨

Lash relaxed, leaning backwards. Teva sat with her back on the arm of the couch they shared. Her toes tucked under his thigh. How tempting the long toes were; he wanted to massage her feet. Instead, he folded his arms.

This was his favorite part of the day, when they were alone

and had nothing to do but rest. "You want some more fruit?" Teva waggled her eyebrows up and down. "I think of Eve every time I ask you that." She held out a bowl full of fruit. No popcorn tonight.

"Eve, huh?" He was in real trouble then. Where she led, he'd follow. He popped a chunk of apple into his mouth.

"So, what's it going to be tonight?" She placed the bowl on the table. "Football, cartoons, or another chick flick?"

"Whatever you want."

The smile she gave him made his heart race. There was something wicked to her look. "Really?"

"Yes."

"Great. I want to play a game."

His lashes lowered. The only game he knew of was one instigated by the legion lords. A lost soul tried to escape the demons. Once caught, the demons always slaughtered and ate their prey. Not always in that order either.

"It's more of a word game. It's called truth or dare." The pulse in her throat sped up. "I think it'll be a nice way for us to get to know each other better."

"Truth or dare?"

"We either answer a question or say dare. If we have to do what's asked."

Sounded simple enough. "If we play, we quit when the clock chimes." He turned more to his right and settled into the corner to see her better. "Since you haven't been sleeping well, you should go to bed early."

"Fine." On a pout, she sighed. "I'll go first, then. What's your favorite area on a woman?"

How one did chose just one area? Salivating, he shifted. No way to get comfortable with his cock constricted by his jeans.

Through lowered lids, he eyed Teva's breasts. Yes, he favored her breasts. He wanted to hold them in his hands and feel them bare against his chest. Next, he eyed her thighs. What he wouldn't give to have them wrapped around his hips.

Sweat broke out on his forehead. He also liked Teva's eyes and her hair. His fingers itched to play in the red curls. "Hmm." He swallowed. His gaze settled on her lips. "I like your mouth best. Especially when you smile."

Just like that, she graced him with one.

There was no stopping the grin that tugged at his mouth in response.

"Wow. Great answer. You sure you haven't played before?"

"I'm sure."

"It's your turn. Ask me anything." She batted her lashes.

"Give me a minute." *Ask her anything.* This was tough. "Okay. Have you ever been married?"

"No, not even close. How tall are you?"

"I don't know." He was much shorter than some of his uncles who'd been cursed to live as giants.

"Can I measure you?"

"Does this count as two questions?" He teased her with a grin.

"No." She shifted and pushed to her feet. "Stand against the wall for me."

Following her guidance, he stood with his back to the wall. Teva pulled a chair over and marked above his head before hopping down. She went back to her desk and returned with a tool he'd not seen before. "Here we go. Help me out here. Hold this end to the mark." She handed him a hooked end of some type of metal. "I'll roll it out for us." She knelt while he lifted his arm to line the hook up with the mark.

Teva straightened. "You can let go now." A flush spread across her cheeks. "Six-five. You would make the perfect football player."

He grunted. He'd learned she had a thing for those players they'd watched. The attraction she had for the football players shouldn't bother him, but it did. Very much so.

Her nose curled. "Are you uncomfortable in the spare bedroom?"

He arched an eyebrow. "Is this another question? You've already had one."

"Sorry." She smiled, not looking the least bit sorry. "Your turn."

They settled back on the couch. He ran an arm along the top of it. "Why haven't you ever married?"

Groaning, she covered her face.

"What?" He caught one of her curls between his fingertips. "You've asked me about a wife and babies. The question seems fair."

"Failures aren't easy to talk about." She wrapped her arms around her folded knees. "Since you really want to know...I've only had three relationships, and none of the guys really cared about me."

"I'm sorry." What fools the men in her life had been.

"Their loss, right?"

"Exactly." In another time and place, he'd have liked to prove to her not all men were fools.

"Tell me about your home. Or at least, what you remember of it."

Lash closed his eyes. His home... Netherworld wasn't fit for her ears. And he couldn't think of what to say about his previous life. The time was so different from the world in which she lived. He hadn't thought about it in ages. Best not to think about what once had been.

The clock chimed, saving him from a dare.

Teva huffed. "It's only one."

"And your alarm starts buzzing..."

"At six." She laughed.

"Ask me questions anytime. If I remember the answer, I'll tell you."

"Okay. Okay." She slid to the end of the cushion. "But I feel cheated. So I want the final answer before bedtime."

"Dare." He swallowed. Teva sat so close now. He could reach out and tweak the hardened nipples taunting him from beneath her t-shirt.

Wide blue eyes blinked. "Oh, um...then I dare you to kiss me goodnight."

"I..."

Turning toward him, she pressed soft curves against him. "It's only a goodnight kiss. It won't do either of us any harm." She leaned closer still to press her mouth to his.

At the feel of her soft lips on his mouth, he groaned.

"Nic," she gasped, "you kiss with your eyes open."

Laughter erupted in his belly, but he stopped it. "You kiss with your eyes closed." He grasped her rounded hips as she clutched at his shoulders. More laughter threatened to burst from inside. He'd never kissed before. And had no clue there was a proper form.

"Oh my God, you laughed." Teva smiled and climbed into his lap. "Close your eyes."

He did as she requested, but opened them at the feel of her breath on his mouth.

"Close your eyes. I want you to feel the kiss."

There was enough to feel with his eyes open. Surely she felt the press of his cock through the layers of their clothes.

Again, he closed his eyes, only to open them when she got close.

"Nic." She laughed.

He smiled. "Fine. But I like watching you."

She caught her lower lip between her teeth and rocked forward along his rigid length. His breath quickened.

Once his eyes closed, she placed her mouth over his mouth. The kiss was gentle. No more than the brush of their lips together. Then she slid off his lap. "Goodnight."

His nostrils flared at the rise and fall of her breasts. "'Night." The sway of her ass kept him captive until she was out of sight.

Kiss with eyes closed. He'd have to remember that rule. Kissing couldn't be too damaging to Teva's soul, though the memories of her sweet mouth would stay with him to torture him once he returned to Netherworld.

CS

Sleep. The guy wanted her to sleep after sharing a kiss. Teva smiled as she pulled back the sheet. Nic was so fine. And she was so hot. How could the guy continue to abstain with the hard package he carried around on a daily basis? She noted his hard-on all the time anymore.

Opening her nightstand drawer, she frowned. It was time to try a new fragrance. "Oh, 'Mystic Nights'." She sniffed the scent. Satisfied, she set it down and picked up the bowl of the potpourri pot. In the bathroom, she cleaned it out to add the new scent.

After adding an inch of oil to the bowl, she placed it on the pot and turned it on to heat. Comfortable in bed, she sighed. Nic had been right, it was late. She didn't know how he functioned with so little sleep.

Sleep came easy; after all, she had Nic waiting in the morning.

A chill slid across Teva's skin as she lifted her head from the cold stone floor. Nearby, a half-woman, half-fish lay on the floor, staring at Teva.

No.

Teva pushed to her hands and knees.

The creature flopped around before legs extended from the back fin. The creature stood as Teva did.

No. No more dreams. No more nightmares.

A pair of glowing eyes appeared behind the fish monster.

Fish-woman smiled to reveal jagged teeth.

Panting, Teva stepped backwards. Torches burst to flames to light up the cavern she stood within. Her head buzzed. She feared she'd faint. Creatures, monsters moved in her direction. A horrible monster with two faces stretched out its grotesque arms to reach for her. Near it, a man with a bull head grabbed his huge cock and stroked. A handsome man leaned over and whispered something into the bull's ear.

Frantic, she turned and fled. On and on she ran. The slap of bare feet, along with the click of hooves, echoed within the walls of the tunnel she dashed down.

She took turn after turn in hopes of escaping the fiends that pursued.

A vibrant orange light grew in the distance. She ran faster toward it. There had to be a way out. She slipped and fell on her stomach, pushing the air from her lungs.

Oh God...

Below her, a river of burning lava rushed past. Her hands clutched at the edge. There was no escape this way. She'd never be able to jump the void to the other side. A whimper slid through her dry lips. If she died before she woke...

Hands grasped her shoulders. "Shh..."

"Nic?"

"I'm here."

"Oh, Nic. Look at them." She glanced back. "They're monsters."

"Get up, Teva. There's no time."

She gulped hot air as he pulled her up. She glanced down at her clothes. Nic was nude. Did she still sleep? Was she dreaming again? Had she brought Nic into her nightmare world? What if they both fell?

He gave her arm a squeeze and jogged off.

Unblinking, she stared at his retreating back. "No. Don't go."

"Be still. They're weak and lazy. They'll never be able to follow us."

He disappeared, only to reappear at a dead run. Her heart pounded. She shook her head in a panic. "No. Nic..." The scream echoed as they sailed across the void. They landed hard on the other side.

Another scream tore from her throat. A monster jumped after them, only to fall into the bubbling lava. Its shattering cry hurt her ears. Over and over, it popped from the river to drop back to the burning liquid.

"Shh. Don't look down there." He urged her up as he stood. "Now, go hide before a winged demon comes along. I'll fight them as long as I can."

"What about him?" She watched as the creature in the lava continued to pop in and out of the river.

"Don't think about him. He'll stay in the river until one of his brothers pulls him out." Then Nic disappeared.

A sob tore from her heart. "Nic."

"Shh." Strong hands gripped her shoulders. "Now, Teva, wake up."

On a gasp, her eyes opened. Dear God...it had been only a dream. She launched herself into Nic's arms. She never wanted to let go again. On a sharp breath, she sucked in a lungful of the musky, fragranced air. Her head swam.

Fear knotted her belly. The nightmare had felt so real.

Chapter Thirteen

Out of sorts, Teva pushed hair away from her face. What was happening to her? Nightmares, of all things. Why now? Sure, her parents hadn't been gone a year yet, but she'd been coping well enough. Her life was fine. Stable.

"You going to eat something?" Nic settled across the table. *Bless him.* He'd prepared French toast and bacon for them. Considering it was nearly noon on Monday, the thoughtful gesture was a great way to kick off the day. At least hers. Nic had already taken care of an arriving camper. And cleaned a recently vacated rental. Sharing responsibilities again was a nice experience.

"Thank you. This is great." How easy it'd be to get used to having him around—and not just for his culinary skills. She licked syrup from her fork before she met his gaze. Oh yeah, for way more than his culinary skills. He looked as fine as ever, with the tight material of his t-shirt across his shoulders and strands of his black hair obscuring his right eye.

"You're welcome. Did you get much sleep this morning?"

"Yeah." Since she hadn't awakened at all during the morning, Nic must've turned her alarm off. She ogled him from beneath her lashes as he ate. He liked the sweet syrup. His tongue flicked out to grab a drop from his lower lip.

She sighed. They'd kissed last night. Probably the greatest kiss of her life. They'd laughed, too. He was great fun, especially when he relaxed. Instinct assured her, vegging out didn't come easily to Nic. Oftentimes, she'd gotten an impression he was on guard, as if expecting something. If only she had more to piece together his intriguing past.

"Think there's a spell in your mom's book for dreamless nights?"

"Oh, I'm sure." She licked syrup from her fingertips. "But, I can't use a spell for personal gain. It's...well, sinful." And a good night's sleep would definitely be for her own benefit.

"Even a spell as simple as one for rest?" He picked his plate up and licked it clean. She didn't have the heart to tell him the act was unmannerly. Instead, she imagined him licking the syrup from her body.

Liquid arousal fired through her body.

You know he wants you.

Teva's heart thumped in her chest.

Use a spell to encourage him to act on his desires.

Her breath quickened.

Or climb up onto the tabletop and spread your eager pussy for him. Watch as he licks syrup from your pussy.

She swallowed.

Imagine his big, hard cock filling up your greedy hole.

"Teva?"

"Huh?" She blinked. God, had she said anything naughty aloud?

"Your face suddenly flushed. You all right?'

A pulse beat in her clit. "I'm fine." But she wasn't fine. What was going on? Had she become a nympho? All she could think about anymore was sex.

Nic regarded her with his endless black eyes a moment before he collected his dishes. She listened as he washed them.

Agitated, she soaked in a bubble bath before going to sit out on the porch. Nic sat with a glass of water in hand. How healthy, to actually drink the recommended allotment of water. She plopped down into a chair beside Nic. Once he drained the glass, he placed it on the wood plank.

"My parents loved it out here."

"I can imagine."

"Believe it or not, there was a time I didn't want to move back here. I'd thought about teaching at a university."

"After your parents…"

"Oh no, when I first went away to college. I let the big city corrupt my upbringing." She sighed. "Just a bit. I thought the country was a place you wanted to visit, not live. I never had many friends growing up. It was too isolated out here. Just me and Mom, mostly."

Intent black eyes regarded her.

"When I finally came home, Dad seemed to be happiest to have me around. Said Mom made him nuts."

"With girl stuff?" A teasing smile flashed to curl her toes.

The guy needed to smile more often. "Tease."

The sexy grin grew. "In my youth, I lived in a lush, fertile valley with mountains that grew into the sky."

"You remember something of your past? Sounds like gorgeous country." She reached over and squeezed his forearm "This is great. Remember anything else?"

He shrugged. "Other things, which I'd rather not recall."

Oh, Nic. Her heart swelled. He was remembering his past.

And a painful one, from the look that had entered his gaze. Nic appeared to have demons lurking—and not in his nightmares, but his memories.

Another yawn. Teva stretched out as best she could on in her corner of the couch. Nic eyed her from his place opposite.

"I'm not tired."

"You keep yawning, and you'll make me start."

On a huff, she blew hair from her eyes. *Shallow Hal* wrapped up on the television. She'd always been a big fan of Jack Black. "What did you think?"

"I think you should go to bed."

"I mean about the movie." Teva rolled onto her back and folded her knees up. At this angle, he probably couldn't see her eyes. They were no doubt slits again. Another yawn attempted to escape, but she fought it back. Fear kept her from sleep. She didn't want any more nightmares.

"I'll take this situation into my own hands." Nic pushed to his feet and scooped her up into his arms before she could scramble out of his reach. "It's late, and you have to sleep. Or I won't see you until dinnertime tomorrow."

She gaped in indignation. "I don't sleep that late."

"Your wake-up hour is growing later and later."

She supposed he was right. She had been getting out of bed later and later. Damn dreams. Tomorrow, she'd get out of bed earlier. Even if she had to crawl.

The arms that held her were strong and comforting. She wrapped her arms around Nic's neck and clung. After inhaling, she sighed blissfully. Now, *his* scent she wanted to bottle. How easy it'd be to sleep surrounded by his masculine smell. She inhaled again.

His arms tightened only a moment before he set her in the middle of her bed. She already missed the contact of his body. She'd noted he'd avoided her touch throughout the day and hadn't made a single move toward her. The arrangement shouldn't get to her, but it did. Badly. The avoidance left her almost depressed.

"Okay. Fine. I'll go to bed."

"Good." A half grin turned a corner of his mouth up. "This way I might see you before noon."

"Oh, stop already." She laughed and scooted over to the nightstand. "Will you rinse this out for me in the bathroom sink? I'm going to try another fragrance out tonight." She cringed. She didn't care a thing for last night's selection. If the oils hadn't been so expensive, she'd toss them out.

Nic sniffed and frowned. "Sure."

She passed over one scent called "Desire's Path". No telling what that one would produce if the nightmare returned. Her heart thumped. Did she truly associate her fragrances with the dreams?

Oh, Teva. Come on. Now she was being silly. The two things couldn't be in correlation. Still, she selected "Night Wishes" to give a go. Once Nic returned, she poured some of the oil and started the heating process.

Adjusting the covers, she settled down on the bed.

"Want me to hang out until you go to sleep?"

"That'd be great." The reply slipped out before she could call it back.

After turning the light out, Nic sat down on the floor with his back against the wall. She started. "Nic, you can't sit down there."

"Why not?"

"Well, because it's got to be uncomfortable."

"It's not."

"It has to be. You're leaning against wood as well as sitting on more wood." She scooted over. "Look, I'm going to be so guilty with you down there, I wouldn't be able to sleep. Lie up here until I drift off. "

Reluctantly, he climbed onto the bed. He folded his arms behind his head as he stretched out on the thin cover. "Happy now?"

"Yeah, I am." She sighed. *Very happy.*

A deep breath rose and fell in his chest. "I don't like your scents you boil."

"Really?"

"Yes. I never lie. Jackson called the one heating the other day peculiar."

She pushed up on her elbow. "Jackson was over here?" Nic hadn't mentioned a visit.

"He stopped over for minute. You were sleeping." Nic crossed his feet. Teva's gaze roamed back up to the bulge from his thick cock that his jeans couldn't hide. "The old man didn't want me to wake you."

"Humph." Of course, she'd been sleeping.

"He had some coffee and offered to help me get identification if I ever want it."

"That's great news." Exciting, really. Her lower lip caught between her teeth as heat rushed to the bundle nerves between her legs. Was Nic thinking of staying around? Now that would be great. She swallowed. She wanted nothing more than to encourage him to stay.

"Did you hear me about Jackson disliking the scent?"

"Yeah." She couldn't help herself changing the subject. "I

think it was very nice of him to offer to help with the identification."

"Something about the scents is bothering me. But, I can't figure out what it is yet."

Sighing, she laid back down. So much for Nic talking about getting ahold of some identification and maybe sticking around a while. "I've been using oils for years now. They're relaxing."

He grunted.

"Well, they are." She blinked. "Nic, you're recalling things. From my studies, I remember scent of smell is the strongest one we have. This is good."

"If I'm remembering something, there's nothing good about the memories." His voice sounded forlorn in the darkness.

Teva wanted to hold him more than anything. Instead, she shut her eyes and willed sleep.

A quick breath rushed between Teva's lips. She peeked through the jagged tear in the stone wall. Below her, an orgy took place. A woman with long blond hair lay on her back. Her head dangled backwards while a handsome blond man shoved his cock in and out of her throat. Across the table, a black-haired man held the woman's thighs up as he thrust in and out of her pussy.

Fascinated, Teva scanned the room once more. In the corner, five men fucked one another in a fucking train. In the other corner, a man sat in a chair as a woman on her knees sucked him off. The woman's hands were tied behind her back while her head bobbed up and down.

Though she knew scenes like this one took place, she'd never thought to witness one.

Back at the table, the men finished with grunts and groans. Two more men replaced the others to fuck the blond-haired woman's pussy and mouth.

Arousal moistened her panties. Never would she have described herself as a voyeur.

"Hello." A voice whispered from behind.

She jumped with a pounding heart.

"You wouldn't like it here."

She glanced around. She could barely see the man in the darkness. Fear settled in her heart at the dim red glow in his eyes.

A monster.

She shook her head wildly.

"Don't fear me. All you have to do is wake up."

She gulped air. Wake up. Wake up. Nothing happened.

"Go on. Get out of here before we're discovered. We've been warned to watch for you."

A desperate urge hit her bladder. The man had been warned about her? Dear God.

"And tell Lash, I owe him no more."

Lash...

Teva woke with a start. Nic slept beside her. Waiting for her heart rate to slow, she worked at dream recall. Nothing useful appeared.

Cautiously, as not to wake Nic, she eased over to his side and pressed her head to his shoulder. When he rolled over in his sleep and took her within his embrace, she nearly cried from the comfort. Something terrible was going on, and all she wanted to do was to solve the puzzle before she lost her sanity.

This closeness couldn't be sinful. Lash caressed Teva's

arm. Her skin was so soft. Not rough and tight like his own. In sleep, she'd cuddled up to his side. She didn't know what he was. Would those in charge of Paradise blame her for allowing him this small token?

Sweat beaded his upper lip. His cock stiffened with need. Lust burned hot in his blood. With his free hand, he pressed along the rigid length hidden within his pants. His balls tightened, and he continued to run his hand back and forth along his cock.

Teva shifted, and he stilled his movements.

"Hmm, I love how you smell." Her hot breath blew across his ear. How she could smell anything other than her oil? He could smell nothing else.

He inhaled sharply at the press of her thigh covering his hard length. Again and again, he sucked in the room's scent.

Teva shifted further. Her breast now fully splayed on his chest.

A shudder racked his frame when her mouth opened against the skin on his throat. "Teva."

"Shhh. There's so much we can do without taking your virginity."

His balls tingled. Over and over, she placed lingering wet kisses on his throat. All he could do was arch in offering. She moaned. Lips nibbled. Her tongue lapped.

His cock pulsed with want.

Another shift had her pussy over his free hand. "Feel that, Nic? Feel how much I want you?" He gulped air. The little pants she wore to bed were wet. Of their own accord, his fingertips ran up the center of the material. Back down, he pressed as far as he could into her hole.

Come boiled in his balls. His hand trembled, with the edge

of a climax approaching. He wanted to bury his cock in her depths. Instead, he worked his fingers over her pussy. The material heated to his touch.

She groaned and rocked her hips. With rough movements, he pressed his fingers along her center. Every time he hit her clit through the material, she sucked on his skin. Just this once. He'd touch her just this once. So he pressed harder, flicking her clit back and forth. His cock jerked every time she uttered a sound of pleasure.

Teva moved up over his throat and chin, until she reached his mouth. The kiss was hot, demanding, as she rocked her pussy on his hand. A time or two, he lost the rhythm he worked to keep on her clit. Lash couldn't breathe. He allowed his fingers to side back down to her hole. Teva ground down on them to bury them as far as they'd penetrate through the barrier.

His hand was damp now from her juices. After thrusting the tips of his fingers in to fuck her as much as he could, he moved back to her clit. Roughly, he rubbed the swollen flesh.

Groaning, Teva sucked his tongue as her body tensed. He rubbed until she broke the kiss, panting for breath. Eagerly she nibbled his lips. "More. I need more."

Her words tore though him. Her need drove Lash. Teva wiggled and arched. He tried to see what she was doing, but couldn't as her lips barely left his mouth while her body shifted away.

At the feel of her bare pussy, his hips arched. Instead of his cock, he buried two fingers within her silken walls. And then inserted a third. Tempted, he wanted to shove his hand in to follow. Teva spread her legs to allow him more room. In and out, his fingers pumped into her slick hole. His thumb slid on her hot spot, and she whimpered.

The sound was caught in his mouth.

Liquid heat pooled on his toying hand. His balls tightened so much he curled his toes. Brutal need shuddered through him. Lungs full, he inhaled the fragrance until its origins settled in his guts.

No! How many times had he been placed in a chamber to have the effects of the unique scent work its magic? Far too often. But those times had been so long ago. Netherworld's scent tainted the air, now that it'd finally registered.

"What?" Teva stilled. "What's wrong?"

She scrambled away to use the covers to shield her body.

"I'm sorry." The scent was used to influence. It was used to weaken. The scent was used to torture until the lost soul folded under the pressure. Somehow, it had made its way into Teva's room. And he'd caved in to his desires.

He sat up and swung his legs over the bed. He inhaled in anger. He hadn't recognized the scent because it was one of the few acceptable smells Netherworld had to offer.

"Oh God, Nic. I didn't mean to...I'm sorry. Don't leave."

Fury knotted his fists as he stood. With quick movements, he removed the containers of oil from the drawer and went into the bathroom. His hands shook while he dumped the bottles into the sink and washed the basin out. Using violent motions, he threw the empty bottles away. "Nic?" Only her voice soothed him. "What's wrong?"

"Let me have the oil bowl."

"Why are you doing this?" She grabbed a small towel and moved back to the bedroom. "Did the scent set off a memory?"

"I can't explain it. I...need to get rid of these scents." He turned his head.

"Okay, if you feel this strongly." She once again wore her

little panto, which barely covered her pussy. She reached out shaky hands, and he plucked up the offered oil bowl. "Careful, it's warm."

With trembling hands, he grasped the bowl tightly. Too tightly, in anger. *How'd she gotten them? More importantly, who'd given them to her?*

He had failed. He'd wanted to protect Teva, and he'd allowed her to use an oil containing an evil element. The bowl broke within his grip. A sharp piece dug into his palm.

Chapter Fourteen

"Oh my God." Teva rushed forward, only to have Nic block her view with his body. Undaunted, she moved around to the other side of the sink. What had gotten into him? And what in the world had come over her? Well, lust had, but still, Nic was abstaining.

"Oh God, you're bleeding." She clasped his rough hands in hers and regarded them. His right hand had a cut in the center of it. His left had a cut in the thumb. "You're going to need stitches." Of that, she was sure.

The wound on his palm split open to ooze more blood as he tried to escape her grasp. As gently as possible, she washed the injuries with soap. Then she ran some cold water over the gash to stop the bleeding. She repeated the same process on his thumb.

Leaving him for a moment, she collected the needed items. She glanced up when she applied the peroxide. He didn't even wince. She'd have been in tears by now. She released a breath. She needed to relax since Nic was so controlled. "Okay, it's clean, but it still needs stitches. Especially this one on your palm." She held his right hand in hers.

"It'll be fine." He closed and opened his hand.

The next blink proved the injuries didn't appear as bad as she'd thought. Strange, there'd been quite a bit of blood. The night played tricks on her eyes. She desperately needed a solid night's sleep.

After getting antibiotic ointment and bandages together, she showed Nic how to care for the small cuts. When she reached for the broken ceramics in the sink, he clasped her wrist. "No. I'll deal with this."

"Nic, you're wearing bandages." She blinked at the look in his gaze. He wouldn't cave on this issue.

"I don't want you handling this." She jerked each time a piece of ceramic landed in the trashcan.

She nodded and allowed the previous hours to invade, or at least, what she could recall of them. She'd come on to Nic in a big way. They'd kissed, and he'd felt her up until she'd come at his touch.

The voices.

Dear God, the voices had encouraged her in each action. And, she'd obeyed them like a puppet.

Then something had caused Nic to pull away. And he'd dumped out all her oils. *All her oils.* A hundred bucks and more in oils. The only thing that kept her mouth shut about the cost was the look that had been on his face as he'd gotten rid of them. His expression had gone from one of fear to one of anger at the shattering of the bowl.

The guy had some serious strength. The bowl had been a nice art piece she'd picked up at a state fair. The piece didn't matter, neither did the oils. Nic meant something to her.

"Don't fear me." Nic pulled her from her musings. He stood tall in the glow of the bathroom light.

Admittedly, there'd been a show of temper, but she had no fear of him. "I don't." The tension remained in his back. "You okay?"

"Yes," He nodded, walked past her and sat on the edge of the bed with his back to her. Teva settled down under the covers. She clutched them so she wouldn't rub his back.

"You must have been pretty upset, you broke the potpourri pot."

"I'm sorry about that. It's just, I remembered something."

"While we were making out?" She winced in both guilt and embarrassment. "About that...I need to explain."

He twisted around to bring a thigh and knee onto the bed. "You've nothing to explain."

"Yes." She rushed on. "Yes, I do. Voices. I've been hearing voices. A female voice."

"What?'

"A female voice. I know this sounds crazy, but she encourages me..." Heat crawled up her neck and face. "I've never behaved with another the way I do with you. It's like she wants me to let go of my inhibitions." A quiver settled in her stomach. There was more, only she couldn't remember what was important.

"Do you recognize the voice?'

"Hmmm." How could she tell him now? "At first, I thought it was me, maybe a double personality or something."

"What?" Puzzlement was clear in his facial expression.

"You know, I thought I was schizophrenic or something. Or had dual personalities." She waved a hand. "I mean, I want to respect your wishes for abstaining, but my subconscious might not." She pushed her hair from her face. "Maybe I need some kind of meds or therapy." What if she was having some sort of a nervous breakdown?

"There's nothing wrong with you, Teva."

She laughed. No way to stop it from bubbling over. "Ah

well, I think after tonight, it's pretty clear something is wrong with me." At least, in her own head.

"Your mind is fine. And I promise you'll have no more dreams now." His rough voice sounded far too confident. Still, she wasn't buying it.

She sighed. "Thank you for the optimism."

"Instincts tell me the feminine voice will disappear, too."

"That would be great, but..." She bunched up her pillow under her head. The voice had somehow been familiar. The familiarity made her unsure. It was as if the voice had a hold on her.

"I don't lie. The dreams will not come again. You let me know if I'm wrong about the voice." Nic stood, bent down and unplugged the bottom of the potpourri pot. She listened as he threw it away in the trashcan.

The light blinked off in the bathroom. Her breath caught at the feel of Nic's weight on the bed behind her. He slid close along her back. Attracted to his warmth, she scooted backwards to make firmer contact. His body was so strong.

Oh, now this is a nice surprise.

"Teva, I'll be here. Go to sleep."

A smile spread across her lips in the darkness. Real pleasure hummed through her body. With Nic here, she would sleep.

Teva slept now. The shallow rise and fall of her chest assured him so. Anger and shame still wielded a heavy weight. Evilness had gotten so close to Teva. Right under Lash's nose. His throat worked. Since being condemned, he'd never come so close to violence before. Had a legion lord or darken appeared during those dark moments, he would have attacked them.

What more could he do?

He rolled onto his back, and Teva snuggled more fully against his chest.

Why hadn't he paid more attention to the hierarchy of the demons? Might there be one among the lords with a shred of decency? What absurdity. Of course, none of them had any decency among them. They'd all gone rotten long ago. Though Zaebos, a Netherworld grand count, was rumored to have a gentle side. The demon lord would surely require a large payment for any assistance given. Payment would be expected when he had none to give.

Did enough magic exist to protect Teva from the dark side? Absently, he played with one of Teva's soft curls. He didn't think so. He doubted even Clauneck, the demon lord over treasures and riches, or Melchom, the treasurer of Netherworld's palace, had enough power to help. And treasures in Netherworld allotted power.

An image of Thoth flashed in his mind's eyes. The being was the demon of magic. If anyone had an answer, it was Thoth. Like the Egyptian would confide in him. Not without a benefit. The false gods were the worst when it came to doling out hate and punishment. Seeking help there would more than likely get him dropped into Netherworld's ocean or volcano for a decade.

The silken threads of Teva's hair slid back and forth between his fingers.

What about a darken? One that held the Prince's favor? He blew out a long, steadying breath. As if one would risk their position.

This is useless. No real help would appear anyway. There was no one.

Teva shifted. "Hm... You're awake." Her voice sounded

husky with sleep. "I can almost hear you thinking."

He grunted.

She rose up silently. "It's nearly three. Have you slept at all?"

"No."

She sighed, snuggling closer. "You should."

"I will." He would, too. At least for a short while. He supposed he didn't require rest, because the lords allowed lost souls so little of it. The only time a lost soul was alone was when they'd been forgotten while being punished. And sleeping was difficult to maintain between deaths. Wait, that was untrue; the newer condemned were permitted to rest while the lords attempted to transform them to darken.

Lash lay still, and after a short while, Teva drifted back to sleep. Tonight's events proved to him that he must try to contact a guardian. Only a sin prevented him from taking the option. Pride. There was no wrapping his mind around a guardian appearing when he called. Lash was among the condemned. Would those in Paradise be amused at his attempt at something as lofty as contacting one among the saved?

Worse, would a demon lord show up at his request instead?

The attempt to contact the guardian would be for Teva's benefit, and he couldn't see another choice. Even if it brought others amusement or brought misery down on himself, Lash had to try to reach out.

He rubbed Teva's back. He wasn't ready to leave her yet. Would never be ready to leave.

Lash waited until he was sure Teva slept soundly. He brushed his lips against her temple and eased from the bed.

Outside, he made his way to his favorite tree and sat down. The sky was wide open. Breathtaking, with all its stars. While missing Teva would break him, he'd also miss Earth. It had been a nice place to visit.

Sweat beaded his chest and forehead. How exactly did one summon a guardian? He'd witnessed many lost souls pray to the Lord of Paradise to no relief, but did one pray to a guardian the same way? Surely Teva's mom would have said if there were special words to utter.

Lash cleared his throat and then did it again once more for good measure. Then he scanned the darkened clearing surrounding him. He was alone, except for the night creatures.

It was now or never. He closed his eyes in prayer.

"I get all the shit assignments."

Lash's eyes opened at the sound of the angry voice. A tall blond man stood in front of him. He was outfitted with an array of weapons, including a sword like the man at the funeral home had been sporting. "Do I get to kick the ass of an incubus who's invaded a beautiful woman's dreams? Or defend some dumbass kid who's accidentally called forth a demon? No." The man's face twisted. "I get summoned by one of the condemned who brings the stink of Netherworld with him."

At least there was no pretense about how the man felt about his kind. Lash stood up. Yes, he preferred to be on even footing with this man.

"Fuck." The man now paced back in forth and muttered in a language Lash couldn't understand.

Lash frowned. He'd been expecting someone more gentle.

"Get to it. Why have I been called here?" The man stopped pacing, only to cross his arms in a defensive manner.

He cleared his throat. "My name is Lash…"

"Your name isn't Lash." The man's face twisted again. Lash had a strong urge to shove his teeth down his throat. He cooled the desire. It wouldn't pay to attack one who was holy or in the position to help Teva. "It's Nicodemus. Now what do you want?"

His teeth clenched. "I would think someone holy like you would be more civil."

"There's nothing holy about me." The man flashed Lash a look. "I'm as cursed as you are. The only difference between us is, I was idiotic enough to ask for justice before I drew my last breath."

"Justice?"

"Oh, yeah, ask for justice as you're dying." The man shook his head in disgust. "It's a kicker. And will get your ass serious hard time in purgatory."

Purgatory. The place had been mentioned among the condemned of Netherworld. "You fight enough demons, you get your soul cleansed of sins?" That seemed fair enough to him.

"No." The man snorted. "I fight evil. I'm doing harm to others. I'm just more fucked."

Now that didn't seem fair. Until he remembered the darkens. They committed sins by participating in the punishments doled out, and they eventually turned demon.

He opened his mouth, but the man held up a hand. "I'm done with this lesson on the afterlife. What does someone in your esteemed position want from me?" The sneer was back in place. "And if you want me to enter Netherworld, the answer is no."

Unable to imagine anyone asking another to enter the world of darkness, he shook his head. "I need you to protect Teva."

"Teva who?"

"Teva Gibson."

"She's not my problem. She belongs under the care of

another in the fellowship."

"What?" The man wouldn't help him. He took a step forward.

Instantly, the sword was out and pressed against his throat. "Don't piss with me."

"Your weapons don't frighten me. No more than death does." His blood turned hot in anger. "Angel, I need your help to protect Teva."

"Am I fucking glowing from goodness? I've already told you, I'm no angel." Easing the sword from Lash's skin, he stepped back. "And your *friend* isn't my problem."

A brutal urge to smash teeth was back in full force. "Who's Teva's guardian? Who can help her?"

The man suddenly pinched his nose as if in discomfort. "Fine. All right." He straightened up. "I've been instructed to be *nice*." He rolled his eyes heavenward. "Nosy sons-a-bitches, I swear." The eyes that met his remained cold. "My name is Dion. Since the only one who can call a guardian is that person, I'll have to see what I can do to help."

Did he dare explain to Teva about guardians? Would she think he'd lost his mind? And just how would he tell how he knew of their existence?

Dion tilted his head backward. "Happy now?"

Above them, a star twinkled brightly.

The guardian snorted. "Archangels." He folded his arms. "Get on with it. What has been happening?"

Lash spent a few minutes filling the man in.

"Her dreams come back, use your powerful psyche to help her to wake. You probably don't remember since you've been damned for so long, but your race is psychic." The man shrugged. "Take me inside, so I can look around."

Lash led the way and resisted the urge to let the door hit the man. *Powerful psyche?* What was the guardian referring to? He simply couldn't recall much of those first decades he'd spent in Netherworld. Only despair and torture had remained a constant.

Dion started in the kitchen. The man sniffed and sniffed more as he went through the house. In Teva's bedroom, Lash made sure the cover hid her tempting body from his visitor. The sentinel spent more time near Teva than anywhere else in the house.

Back outside, the blond noisily exhaled. "You're fucked. She's fucked. Everybody's fucked. And not an ounce of pleasure involved. Damn shame." Dion shook his head. "I caught a few lingering scents, but it's not demons who mean your friend harm. It's a human."

"So?" Lash folded his arms. "So what?" He didn't care who meant Teva harm, he just wanted the threat stopped. The hair prickled his on his forearms. Clarisse. Clarisse meant Teva harm. His instincts had been on the mark. And she'd been the one to put the impurity in the oils Teva regularly used.

"Pal, I can behead all the demons my happy ass wants. But, I fuck up a human...I do not pass go. I go straight to Hell." The man smiled as if amused with himself. "Now you, on the other hand. You're already condemned." Dion shrugged. "Take the human out. It makes no difference to me."

A jagged streak of lightning burst across the clear night sky.

"Over-sensitive eavesdroppers." He sighed. "Don't pay my encouragement any mind." He winked.

Lash's pulse accelerated. Could more be done to him than what had already been meted out in Netherworld? After the streak of lightning, he guessed there was that chance.

"All right, look." Dion rubbed his hands together. "Your friend gives a shout out for help, I'll come to her aid. I'll find out which among the fellowship has been put in charge of her care and make a trade-off." The sentinel glanced upward. "You know, I deserve my fucking wings for all this niceness."

Wind blew roughly between them, as if sighing.

Lash grunted. This man was going to come to Teva's aid? His faith took a deep dip.

"Okay, if that's it?" Dion clapped. "I'm outta here." In a blink, the man disappeared into thin air.

He was left with little comfort from the visit. Somehow, he had to convince Teva how truly evil Clarisse had turned. Maybe there was a spell within her mom's book that would offer protection.

His eyes closed, and his fist clenched as he recalled Teva's words. *Magic couldn't be used for your own benefit.* At least, not good magic.

The sentinel was right. At that moment, they were all fucked.

Chapter Fifteen

The day had been a peaceful one after a rather restless night. Now she tossed the last of the needed herbs into the goulash. Teva moved away from the door at the sound of a car pulling up. Nic had gone to the cabins to help out a camper who'd gotten his truck stuck in the mud. Her lip caught between her teeth. Though he shouldn't be driving without a license, as it was illegal, she hadn't hesitated loaning him her jeep. A tiny part of her had worried he might just take off. Her jeep wasn't even three years old. Someone might give him a nice bit of change for the automobile. She hadn't expected him back so soon.

Her heart raced in excitement as she moved to open the door for Nic. The more he settled into her routine, the more attached she got. She couldn't separate the attraction from the attachment anymore.

Dread replaced the excitement at the sight of her aunt approaching the porch. Her hands tightened on the door as if to slam it shut.

Heck and damn. No way did she want to deal with her aunt today, or ever. The unease intensified. "Hello, dear." Clarisse kissed her cheek as she passed through the open door. Teva wanted to wipe the show of affection away.

"Hey. This is a surprise, and so soon after your last visit." Teva scrutinized her aunt. Today, while the woman was dressed as perfectly as before in a black tunic and dress slacks, her face was tense. Her green eyes looked duller. Teva blinked. Did she see the fine lines of wrinkles on Clarisse's forehead?

"Yes, I know. I was in the city and thought since we've begun anew with our relationship, I'd drop in."

Teva looked away. She couldn't recall agreeing to begin anew in anything with Clarisse, and after her mom's letter...

Clarisse glided to the table. "Besides, I have a few things of your mother's I thought you'd appreciate." Once she'd sat down, she handed over a designer shopping bag.

Teva's breath caught. She grasped the handles with white knuckles. Was Clarisse up to something? Did she actually have items that had belonged to her mom? Better yet, had they been important to her mom?

"Dear, did my gift arrive?"

Teva met the other woman's eyes. "Yes. Thank you. It's lovely."

"I see you're not wearing it."

"Hmm." She pulled the bag apart. "It's too fancy for everyday wear." There, that lie should cover the disappearance. She didn't know how she'd handle it if her aunt pushed the matter. She'd thrown the crushed bracelet in the trash and couldn't say what Nic had told her to. Though he had pleased her with his protectiveness.

Thankfully, Clarisse didn't pry further. "The bag holds some of Gina's childhood treasures."

Teva inhaled sharply as she pulled a lovely baby doll from the bag. Gently, she laid the doll atop the table. Next, she pulled out doll clothes and a silver mirror set.

"That set used to be our mother's."

"You want to get rid of these?" She ran her hand over the doll clothes.

Clarisse's slim shoulders rose and fell in a shrug. "Well, Teva, I am getting older, and I have no children to give them to."

She supposed Clarisse was lonely, and Teva couldn't stop herself from feeling sorry for the older woman. Teva missed her parents so much. What must it be like for Clarisse, to have no one to rely on or even share holidays with?

"Hold on. I think there's one remaining item in the bag." Clarisse waved a manicured hand.

Teva plucked a long pearl necklace from the bag's depths. Lastly, two doll dresses followed. She laid the dresses on the table while she examined the necklace. The pearls had a nice weight to them. They must be real.

"The necklace dates back to the 1920's. Not sure how your mom came to have them. But long beads and pearls were the rage back then."

What year were flappers popular? Teva tried, but couldn't pull forth the trivia. "These are great." The items were truly beautiful. And if there was a chance they'd once belonged to her mom, she could pass them on to her own daughter. Well, if she ever had one. The memory of Nic collecting the toy for the baby in the grocery store surfaced. He'd be so good with a child. She sighed. "Thank you."

"I'm sorry. I can't stay long this trip."

"Oh, that's okay."

"I'm old though, and I need to make a trip to the bathroom before I head back."

"Sure." She caressed the smooth pearls.

Later, she'd have to go through the old photos and see if

she could find the belongings anywhere. More than anything, she wanted to know if the keepsakes had belonged to her mom. She sighed and placed the necklace around her neck. She tied the pearls in a knot. After a moment of admiring the pearls, she removed them. Standing, she walked over to a basket and hid the pearls inside. She replaced the decorative lid to keep the dust off them.

What to do with the doll and clothes? The mirror set, she'd lay out in the guestroom. She didn't pay much attention to her aunt until the woman left Teva's bedroom. Teva narrowed her gaze. Clarisse had used her bathroom again.

The hair along her arms prickled, and she glanced back at the basket where she'd hidden the jewelry.

"I noticed your home doesn't..." Clarisse pursed her lips. "...still have that lovely scent from my last visit."

Nervously, Teva's tongue darted out to moisten her lips. Unease crawled up her spine. "Oh, I recently developed headaches from the therapeutic oils." God, that sounded lame. She wiped her sweaty hands on her shorts.

Clarisse kissed her cheek goodbye. "Well, don't worry. I'm sure the headaches will disappear now." Her aunt's smile creeped her out. She rubbed her arms. "I'll be in touch, dear."

"Drive safe."

The door closed with a soft click. Turning, Teva caught sight of the unblinking doll. She frowned. She hadn't noticed how green the doll's eyes appeared before. Or how real they looked.

CB

Lash scratched his head. The two men had only gotten

their truck stuck deeper during the time he'd watched their dilemma. One drove. One pushed. Tires spun, going nowhere.

The boards Teva had suggested before he left didn't do the trick. Mud sprayed everywhere.

He shook his head. Teva had said they'd probably taken a vehicle that wasn't designed for off-roading onto her dirt trails. She'd explained only four-wheel drives and a good suspension worked out here to get you from one point to another.

Though he didn't understand it all, he believed a difference between off- and on-road vehicles existed. These men didn't have an off-road vehicle.

Life circumstances kept him quiet. In Netherworld, he only spoke if spoken to. Since his arrival at Teva's, he hadn't been much of a talker. Old habits die hard. Unsure on how to approach the men with a suggestion, he hung back.

More mud splattered and rubber burned before the men finally gave up.

Lash rocked back on his heels.

The man named Ed climbed out of the truck carrying three bottles. "What a bitch. I hate mud. Have a beer." He passed around the bottles. Ed twisted the cap and took a long swallow.

Lash followed suit and pinched his nose at the head rush.

Ed laughed. "Nothing beats a cold beer."

"I can think of a few things." Jerry snickered.

On the fourth swallow, Lash had the harsh taste memorized. He preferred water. The bottle drained, he handed it back. "Thank you." He bit back a burp. "You want me to push?"

Jerry laughed. "Didn't think you'd ever offer." Jerry set his beer down on a flat stone. They walked over to the back as Ed climbed back inside the vehicle.

The truck roared to life with spinning tires. Mud flew

everywhere. He grasped the back of the truck and lifted. Lash put strength into his arms and shoulders to give a hard push. The truck moved forward, and Jerry fell flat on his face in the mud.

Lash blinked down at the sputtering man.

"Holy shit. You're strong as a bull."

Lash grunted. *A bull.* He hadn't worked up a sweat, though he was now filthy. Long strides brought him out of the hole.

Ed climbed out of the truck and handed him another bottle. "Thanks, man." They exchanged a nod before the man climbed back inside.

Twisting the cap, Lash removed the lid. He drank down the liquid in a long swallow before he wiped his mouth. Now, to get back to Teva's covered in mud. He used the blanket she kept in the back of the truck to save her seat from the mess.

Back at Teva's, he used the water hose attached to her home. He sprayed the mud from his hands, arms, boots, and head. Teva came outside and put a pair of his shorts on a chair. "Have fun?"

Lazily, he took in every curve of her lush body and sucked in a breath as arousal ignited in his blood. "The truck they had isn't fit for off road." His head buzzed a little from the beers. He'd never been inside Netherworld's gaming halls, where alcohol still held some captive.

"See?" She grinned. "Dinner will be ready soon." Her curls bounced as she turned and went back through the doorway.

He shivered at the cold water. Since his clothes were still dirty, he stripped on the porch and stepped into the shorts, stuffing his semi-erect cock inside. Teva always turned him on.

He took his usual chair at the table. Teva's face already had a high flush. His cock hardened more. Underneath the table, he rubbed the rigid length.

Teva's eyes were dark. He'd often seen that look when she got aroused. He cupped his balls. Squeezed his cock.

"Nic, you want some water?"

"Water." He needed water to help cool down. "Yes, thanks." Not that it would do much.

Her ass swayed as she walked to the sink.

He inhaled, his mind still hazy from the beer. He needed to cool it. Needed to think clearly.

"Here you go." She placed the glass in front of him. Across the table from him, she sat down.

His instincts went on alert. She was agitated. No, probably as turned on as he was. "You all right?"

"Oh, yeah." Her smile did more than reassure him.

Releasing his cock, he placed his hands on the table.

Teva's own hands disappeared beneath the table. Her lip caught between her teeth.

Need curled deep. He closed his eyes. Was she playing with herself as he had?

Lash inhaled sharply at the feel of her hands on his thighs. She'd crawled under the table and settled between his legs.

A groan vibrated in his chest, and his head dropped back. He grabbed the table edge as she lowered the waistband to get to his cock. She pushed the material under his sac causing him to jerk at the added pressure.

A wet tongue slid up from his balls along the center of his cock. A hot mouth circled and screwed down over its head.

Lash moaned at the sensations building. She licked him like he was a favorite treat. Over and over, her eager tongue ran up and down his length. Every now and then, she sucked a side of his sac into her mouth. He jerked every time.

He couldn't take it. No one had ever touched him in such a way. He craved more. His balls tightened in anticipation of the rising pleasure.

White-knuckled, his fists hit the table at the feel of her hand grasping him. She pulled his cock away from his body so she could sink her wet mouth over the length. She slurped as the suction moved up and down.

Again he dropped his head back. The haze buzzed in his mind. He spread his legs and thrust his hips up.

Teva moaned and sucked harder. Her teeth scraped. He nearly came.

No. Not yet.

He shook his head. Not yet. His balls tightened, yet she sucked harder. Her fist pumped up to meet her downward sliding lips.

He groaned. Shifted his hips.

Savage need tore through him. "Teva." His body tensed. His cock pulsed at the streams of come erupting into her slurping mouth.

Teva stayed with his cock until the last drop had emptied. Only then, did his mind clear.

Lash's head dropped forward in guilt. What had come over him? He should have stopped her.

She tucked his cock back in before coming out from under the table. Her face flushed from arousal. Her eyes were so dark with passion they appeared almost black. "See, I told you there are all kinds of things we can do without taking your virginity."

A chill set the hairs on the back of his neck on end. *Something had happened.*

Lash stood as he raked his hands through his hair. What utter lack of control on his part. Panic was clear in her eyes now. Quickly, he moved around the table to squat on his haunches beside her. "Teva?"

"Dear God, the voice came back."

He growled. How could that be? He'd assured himself the oils had been the danger.

"I don't know what came over me." Her hands covered her face and muffled her voice. "I've never ever done anything like that."

The admission tightened his chest. Not that it'd matter, but the fact pleased him. A grin turned his mouth up. "It was a first for me, too."

She gasped and peeked through two fingers at him.

"Don't...don't be embarrassed. You had me so hot. It was ..." Remarkable. He'd never forget her mouth on him. Her tongue caressing him. Or her throat drinking him down. "Tell me what happened today." He hadn't expected the voice to return anymore than he had the damn dreams. How could he have been so wrong?

"I..." Nervously, she moistened her swollen lips. "I had a visit from Clarisse."

"What?" He stood, his fists clenched by his side. "Why? What did she do while she was here?" His mouth twisted. "Did she give you another blessing?"

She rubbed her arms as if she was cold. He wanted to comfort her, but he had to get rid of whatever the evil woman had bought inside.

She sighed. "Nothing. Really, she stopped by for only a few minutes. She brought a few things which used to be my mom's."

His heart thumped in his chest. The woman wouldn't dare to use Teva's mom against her. He growled out of disgust at Clarisse's actions. Of course she would. Without a second thought. "Where are they?"

Teva jerked at his tone.

Lash exhaled to calm himself down. It wasn't working. "What did she bring?" Air rushed in and out of his nose as his chest heaved in anger. "Teva, that woman means you harm."

"She said they used to be my mom's."

"Of course she did. How much easier to get you to accept them?"

With shaky hands, she pushed her hair back from her face and stood up. "I don't know. She seemed sincere."

"She seemed sincere, or you wanted her to be sincere?" He looked around the room for anything new or out of place. "The woman is conniving and manipulative."

"I don't know." Her voice had weakened.

"The gifts got her inside to try and harm you once more." Unable to stop himself, he grasped her upper arms. "Come on. If you don't believe me, read your mom's letter again."

Tears filled her eyes. "How could she? If the keepsakes belonged to Mom, I want to keep them."

Groaning, he pulled her into his arms. Her head rested on his shoulder. Her arms wrapped tightly around his middle. He massaged her back and simply held her for a few minutes until the trembling stopped in her body.

He released her to collect her mom's spell book. He retrieved the letter and unfolded it. "I want you to read this." When he got rid of the stuff Clarisse had brought, he wanted Teva's mom on his side.

"Of course, you're right." She handed the letter back to

him. And he stored it away in its safe spot.

"I need you to walk me through her steps and show me what she left behind."

Shoulders drooped, Teva turned around. "She sat here at the table and went to the bathroom." Her eyes rounded. "My bathroom."

"You saw her in there?"

"Well, no, I saw her come out of my room." A pained look crossed her face. "And I saw her come out of my bathroom last time. Shit. I thought it was odd at the time. She knows where the spare bedroom is..."

The bitch. He grabbed a trash bag before he left the area. Moving past Teva, he went to her bathroom, where he threw out all the liquids.

"Is this necessary?" She reached for a small glass bottle he was trashing.

He held the container out of her reach. "It's best to be careful, rather than sorry." Though he might be overreacting, he didn't know how much time he had. Incidents had been escalating. He wanted to do what he could while he was still here.

She pushed her hair back. "I can't believe this."

In the bedroom, he tossed the lotion she used on her skin into the bag as well.

Teva groaned and plopped onto the bed. "I *really* can't believe this."

Lash allowed her thighs to distract him. Often, he watched her apply lotion to her legs. Lust stirred. He shook the arousal off. "Where are the offerings?"

"The doll and its clothes." She pointed to a small red-haired being on the chair in the corner. He'd never seen such a thing.

Without hesitation, he added it to the trash. The stack of little clothes followed.

Noting the longing in her eyes, his fist tightened around the bag. "Teva, how do we know this couldn't be dangerous to others?" He could see a small child cradling the pretend baby. Of course, Teva would want to give it to her child if it had actually belonged to her mom. He caressed her cheek. "You're doing the right thing. Your mom would want you and yours safe."

Her gentle smiled soothed him. "I know. Come on, let's get the rest."

In the room he used, she plunked a mirror and comb into the bag. And, last went some sort of jewelry.

"This is it?"

"Yep."

Satisfied, he nodded. "All right, I'll take this outside to the trash can, then."

"Thanks, Nic."

"You up for a chick flick?" He tried for a grin.

The suggestion had the desired effect. Teva laughed. "You hate them. I know you do."

Well, he wasn't crazy about them, but he'd take the memory of spending more time with Teva.

Chapter Sixteen

Teva uncrossed her legs and pushed rewind on the old VCR. The past couple of hours had been immensely relaxing. She and Nic had gotten a kick out of *Rush Hour*, though she'd already seen it a half-dozen times. Nothing like a good action comedy to take the edge off. And she'd discovered Nic's favorite movie genre. She'd love to get him into a comedy club. She loved to hear his laughter. "What'd you think?"

"Better than chick flicks."

"Hey, I love those." She whapped him with a pillow. "I own part two, too. Wanna watch it?'

"No." Holding the pillow, he stretched back on the couch and placed it behind his head. Teva forced herself not to scroll her eyes down his body to check out his package. "I'm thinking maybe I can do one of your mom's spells."

Now, *that* she hadn't expected. "Hmmm, I'm not sure that'd work. I mean, you've never practiced magic before, have you?" Had he remembered something new? "I'm just a novice myself. If that." She'd doubted herself.

"I want to try." Nic sounded firm.

"Spells are prayers in a sense. Many practitioners use them to create needed change. But while prayers are a petition to an external magic to create the change, we Celts believe that magic is present in everything, including ourselves." She held his intense gaze. He was serious about this. "Spells, then, are the channeling of our own energies, to create the change."

"The magic comes from within," Nic murmured, more to himself then to her.

"Yeah, so you understand, since you've never harnessed your magic before..."

"I believe in this case, I can pray with as much focus as another." His hair fell over his left eye as he shifted. "You said magic can't be used to benefit yourself, but I have the right to try a spell to protect you."

"Well, technically, yes." She'd never known anyone who wanted to work a spell out of the blue, but then, she remembered once in high school a few classmates had dared each other into taking a turn around a Ouija board. And it wasn't like she was trying to convert Nic to the pagan beliefs. He'd brought the spell up. She shrugged. "Why not?" After all, pagans believed in free will and free choice.

"Can you find me a spell and teach me the words?" Nic sat up straight.

"Sure. And we've got a quarter-moon outside tonight. So that's a bonus." She got her mom's spell journal out and sat on the floor by the coffee table while Nic went and got himself some water.

Rejoining her, he sat on the floor near her with his long legs outstretched.

"You want to listen to some music?"

"If you like."

Teva tossed him a stereo controller. "Well, here, you find us something." She'd quickly learned he didn't care for her heavy metal. He'd turned it down too many times.

She hid her smile and opened the book as Nic pressed play.

He liked gadgets and was pretty damn good at figuring them all out on his own. Or his memory had returned on certain aspects.

Elvis sounded from the speakers. Nic's feet swayed to the rhythm of "Jailhouse Rock".

She bit back a wince. She'd created a monster. He liked Buddy Holly, too. Golden oldies wasn't her genre.

She sighed and flipped the book to where she'd left off. The journal was huge, with hundreds of entries.

An old Johnny Cash song played when she finally looked up. "I found a spell that had once been used to protect a castle in Ireland during the 14th century." It was a neat legend. One of her ancestors had included a lot of the legend's details in the tale. On the older spells, a tale was told, then, it listed the actual spell. She puckered her lips. Why hadn't Clarisse ever tried to get her hands on this? Surely, somehow she could have twisted the spells to suit her own needs.

"I need one that protects individuals, too." He fingered the wood clover she'd given him as a blessed charm. "Never mind. That spell will do fine." A look she didn't understand or like entered his gaze. Sad. Desolate. He was the first to look away to surf for more golden oldies.

"Enjoy your songs. I'll look a bit more."

He teased her with one of his sexy half smiles. "Now this is great music."

She giggled. "If you say so." She was still smiling as she turned the page. "I guess if those guys hadn't come along when they had, I wouldn't have my favorites." She blew a curl away from her eyes. "Everything in life happens for a reason."

"Yes, Teva, it does."

Skimming, she turned a page. Then another. So much to

comb through.

Bill Haley's "Rock Around The Clock" belted out, and Teva wanted nothing more than to take Nic to an old fashioned drive-in movie. Neat, how one thing led to another. But Nic would've gotten a kick out of being at a drive-in. And so would she, if she could have gotten him into the backseat. She squirmed. *Focus, woman.*

Through tunes by Chuck Berry, Fats Domino, The Everly Brothers and nameless others, Teva skimmed in search of the right spell. Her mind kept returning to the one centered on the ancient castle. Something about it appealed to her. "This spell is to protect my home?"

"Yes." His black eyes bored into hers. Determination flamed within their depths. At least he was confident. And, she should be, too. She flipped back twenty-some pages.

Teva tapped a fingernail on the page. "Okay, I say you go with this spell. "

The music disappeared. "Do we need anything special for it?"

"Just prayer words and energy."

"And faith." He stood up and offered her his hand. A jolt of attraction ran through her body. She scrunched her legs together.

"Great. How about I collect the makings for some s'mores? We can melt them in the bonfire after the spell casting."

"S'mores?"

"Oh, they're better than French toast."

Nic's sexy grin tilted the right side of his mouth up. She quivered. God, she loved his smile.

Flames of gold and butter-yellows meshed with oranges and reds within the bonfire. The pop and snap of the fire blazed as smoke continued to rise into the night sky. Pagans tended to hold ceremonies or "circles" outdoors, to bring them closer to the divinity who created the world. Under the moon was an even more powerful position. Maybe luck would be on their side, too. Especially since she had no clue what her aunt had against her.

Nic stood tall and proud near the blaze. He'd long since offered his words to bring about the spell. Still, he continued to stand as if in prayer. She remained silent to give him as much time as he needed.

Sighing, she wrapped her arms around bent knees. The flames streaked up into the sky. This magic had been so important to her mom, her grandmother. How could she have turned her back on that heritage?

Yes, Mom hadn't wanted her to take the path, but there had been such wrongness in her lack of commitment. No more. Teva closed her eyes. Earthy scents of smoke, dirt, and stagnant water filled her senses. Clarisse had embraced the dark side of magic, but her mom had never been tempted. And neither would she. She understood the favor of good.

As soon as she could, she'd track down members of her mom's old coven. They'd be able to teach her the path of magic. She'd bet willingly, too.

Nic shifted his arm up to clasp the charm he wore around his neck.

She didn't understand his action. She'd already spoken over the four-leaf clover. For a long while, Nic stood still, until he walked over to join her on the blanket she'd brought outside.

"Ready for your first s'mores?"

"Yes." He placed his palm on his bent knee.

"Great." She got the chocolate and graham cracker ready before she withdrew marshmallow from another storage bag. "Okay, first we melt these puppies."

He frowned, but took the offered utensil and shoved several marshmallows onto the tongs. "These don't look like puppies."

"Oh, well, no." She laughed. "Sorry. Figure of speech. Okay, now stick them above the flames until they get nice and gooey." She passed him hers, so she could bag everything back up. "Gosh, these are going to be so good. It's been a long time since I've done this."

The flames licked at the sweet treats.

"Thank you." Their fingers touched as she took back her long fork.

"You're welcome. Better than French toast, huh?"

"Oh, yeah. You just wait."

The marshmallow didn't take long to melt to perfection. Teva licked her lips when she pulled the treats from the flames. Nic withdrew his fork, too.

"Next, we slap these babies between these crackers and chocolate."

Nic tested the marshmallow with his fingers.

"Careful, they're hot."

He didn't seem to notice as he brought a smidgen to his mouth. He closed his eyes. "It's good. Sweet."

"See, but it gets better." She worked her marshmallows off the tongs and onto her cracker. "Now, make your sandwich." After placing her s'mores on a spare storage bag, she collected everything and reached for his fork. "I'm going to put these in some soapy water to soak, while mine cools."

He nodded, already nibbling on his dessert.

Chore complete, she settled back down beside Nic on the blanket. "So, what do you think?"

"I think you were right." He licked his fingers clean.

"I told you they were great." She extended hers toward his mouth. "Want some of mine?'

"You sure?"

"Yep. Have a bite." Like she needed the calories.

She blinked at the giant chunk he took. And then she laughed. "Wow, you have a big mouth."

"I thought I'd better take a big bite in case that's all I was offered." He licked his lips.

Teva laughed easily. The guy was so honest. "Here, have another. We can make more."

Nic took a smaller bite. "Thank you for sharing, but we don't have to make more. Unless you want to."

"One is enough for me." They could be overly sweet, especially since they'd each used a full bar of chocolate. "But are you sure?"

She should've asked him before putting everything away. She'd been used to eating them with her mom. One had always been enough for them.

"Yes, I'm sure." His hair fell across his face, shielding his gaze.

She offered him her last bite. His lips sucked her fingers into his mouth along with the treat. She gasped, quivering in pleasure as the suction raced all the way to her sex.

Nic kept sucking her fingers until he caught her wrist in his rough palm. Her heart beat wildly. He placed a kiss in the center of her hand. His lips traveled along her wrist and up her arm. She couldn't think, only shift closer to him.

"Ooh..." She moaned and tilted her head to the side when

he reached her shoulder. A rush of liquid desire dampened her panties. How long had she wanted this? Wanted Nic. Warm lips and a wet tongue played across her skin. "Oh..." No way to catch her breath. She panted. Sweet sensations burst with every touch of his mouth. The trembling in her body increased with every caress of his hands.

A delicious need pulsed in her center. Teva clutched at his strong shoulders as he laid her back on the blanket and claimed her mouth in what had to be the hottest kiss of her life. She enjoyed the lingering taste of chocolate as much as she enjoyed the heat of his mouth devouring hers. His hunger curled her toes and arched her hips.

Nic's tongue relentlessly stroked and teased with hers to play in-between nibbles of his teeth on her lips. She clasped his face. Over and over, her hips arched to rub his rigid cock.

Teva whimpered; she couldn't hit the right spot. She shifted to cradle him between her thighs. His hips thrust forward to slide his cock along her pelvis. She gasped into his hungry mouth. The pulsing need in her clit heated. She whimpered as more wetness flowed.

She wanted her sex filled up. Filled up with him. "Oh, Nic..."

"I want you," Nic rasped between kisses. "I want you so badly."

With a pounding heart, Teva stilled.

"I want you, Teva." Nic caressed her flushed cheek.

"Are you sure?" she whispered on a panted breath. "I mean, I'm very sure, but are you sure?"

He placed a gentle kiss on her swollen mouth. "Yes, I'm sure." Now that he'd cast the spell she'd be safe. Safe from even the repercussions their loving might have. He had to hold her, touch her. Become one with her, even for a little while.

He shifted over so he could see Teva's body in the firelight. Her hair flashed fire. Her blue eyes had darkened. Her thighs appeared almost white in the semi darkness. And her breasts now displayed peaks beneath her thin shirt.

Lovely.

He planned to memorize her every curve tonight. Every inch. He'd take this night with him tomorrow. The moments with Teva would be treasured for the rest of his eternity. No longer would he play a part in Teva's destruction. He'd force the lords to teleport him back to Netherworld where he belonged.

But tonight would be theirs.

Lash dipped his head to claim her lips once more. He savored every bit of sweetness. Every sigh. With trembling fingers, he cupped her breast and massaged. He plucked at the hardened nipple beneath the cloth. The firmness of her flesh fit his palm perfectly.

Teva's hand drifted from his shoulders to tangle in his hair. The tugs to get him to deepen the kiss incited his hunger. Need rushed through his blood.

Her supple thigh rose up to rub along his own. Her hips arched as he pinched her nipple.

Lash's breathing rushed harshly through his nose. He needed air. He wanted to take things slowly. Memorize every detail. He would find the strength to take his time.

Letting go of her breast, he slid his hand under her top. He wanted to touch her skin. Wanted to look his fill. At the feel of his hand caressing her stomach, Teva whimpered and broke the kiss. "Oh, let me get this off." She wiggled. He allowed her a little room to remove her shirt. His cock jerked at the sight of her bare breasts.

Flat on her back, Teva squeezed her breasts in her palms. Lash swallowed and lowered his head to suckle on the nearest nipple.

She moaned, continuing to squeeze her free breast. The pressure in his balls intensified. His head hummed with the need to come.

Licking his way across to her other breast, he claimed the nipple. He sucked hard. Teva arched on a moan. She gripped his hair. He was unsure if she was urging him to suck harder or to stop the suction. So he sucked harder until her cry broke the night.

Frantically, her thigh rubbed along his hip as she tried to add pressure to her clit. She wanted him to fuck her. He wanted that even more. Instead, he moved back to her other breast and nipped at her fingers that toyed with the nipple.

Tonguing her fingertips out of the way, he sucked the nipple deep into his mouth. She cried out and quivered.

Lash slid his hand down her stomach and into the short pants she wore. Then, he buried his hand beneath the little panties she wore underneath. Her pussy was wet.

"Oh God, let me..." She wiggled as her hands scrambled down to push at the waistband. He refused to break the contact on her nipple.

Teva thrust her hips up on a cry. He pushed at the short pants with her until she had them down low enough to work her legs out of them. Only then did he lift his face from her breast.

So lovely.

She wasn't shy, she spread her legs wide. She threw one of her thighs over his hip to give him all the room he needed.

Her body scorched his. He wanted his clothes off, but kept

control on his hunger, his need.

He trailed his fingers down her stomach and watched it quiver at his touch. When he reached the curls that hid her pussy, she reached down and pulled her other leg up.

Lash's hips jerked at the sight of her splayed pussy. His mouth went dry. His fingers trailed past her clit. Teva moaned. He allowed a single finger to disappear. She lifted her head to watch as well, though only briefly before dropping it back, reacting to the slow pumping action of his finger.

His balls tingled in anticipation of flooding her depths with his hot come. A second finger joined the first. The muscles in his hand and arm flexed as he worked the digits in and out. At the tensing in Teva's body, he withdrew his slippery fingers and toyed with her clit.

Rolling her head side to side, she whimpered. The muscle on his forearm caught between her clenched fingers. Her lip caught between her teeth. Quickly, he added more pressure to the swollen flesh that stuck outwards for his attention.

Teva's nails dug into his arm while she clenched in climax. Her cry lingered in the night.

Harsh breaths rushed from his nose. He shifted to his knees to remove his straining cock from his jeans.

Teva hand replaced his own as she rubbed at her clit in his absence.

He winced when he was free of the confinement. He shifted his jeans down until his balls were free as well. He squeezed them. Stroked his cock a time or two as he watched Teva at play.

So lovely. If only you were mine.

Grasping her ankles, he moved up between her thighs. Teva pulled her pussy wide with her fingertips. It was an invitation he couldn't resist. He wedged his cock into her wet hole. Slowly, the rigid flesh disappeared into her pussy. He sucked in a breath at the feel of her ass slapping his balls.

"Give me more." She squeezed her breast.

He kissed her ankles, earning sounds of pleasure. She brought a hand down to where their bodies joined and flicked her clit before rubbing his exposed cock.

Pushing forward, he brought her legs with him until her ankles hung at his shoulders. She trembled. Pinched her nipples. Then his. Lash's hips jerked. Braced on his hands, he thrust his hips to drive his cock in deep.

A moan escaped her lips with each pump of his cock. His hip action turned brutal. Sweat coated his body. Teva grasped his wrists for leverage so she could rock her hips up. Time after time, his balls slammed into her ass to bring him one thrust closer to climax.

Wet heat engulfed him as her pussy walls encased his cock. Brutally, he fucked Teva. Harder and faster, he worked hips and ass to earn cries of passion. Only when the sweet ache of her quivering inner pussy walls milking him became too much, did he unload. He groaned while his hot come burst out to spray deep inside.

Chest heaving, he released Teva's legs to collapse on her. His cock was still buried deep. Teva trembled. "Oh, Nic." She clung tight. "God, that was great."

He didn't have enough air yet to respond, so he nodded. He hadn't known it'd be that way. It was better than great. His cock thickened within her clenching muscles.

"Oh, I'm all for more, but I say let's head to bed." She tightened her arms around his neck. "I think my spine was bruised."

He grunted. Damn, he hadn't been thinking too clearly.

Melissa Lopez

Lord, he would miss her.

Chapter Seventeen

Lash grunted, though the couch cushioned them as they tumbled down. Teva helped to remove his clothes and urged him to lean back. Trembling hands splayed on his chest. She straddled his hips. After teasing his cock with her wet pussy, she impaled herself on his hard length.

Bracing his feet on the floor, he thrust his hips up to stroke deeper. His hands grasped her hips as she rocked back and forth. Lash's neck arched.

Sweat broke out on his chest. Too fast. His control was slipping way too fast.

Teva moaned and ground her hot, gripping pussy on his buried cock. Her breasts bobbed with her every movement. Salivating, he urged her to bring a nipple to his mouth. She refused. Only rode him harder.

He groaned. His sensitive balls tingled at the feel of her dripping juices.

Up and down she slid as her flushed breasts heaved. Her nipples begged for his touch. He could do no more than hang on to Teva's driving hips as she sought to quench her own need.

The moment her pussy convulsed in climax, he lunged up a final time. His come burst out at Teva's hoarse cry.

His body tensed. Jerked while the stream of come filled Teva's hole.

Weak and panting, she collapsed on his chest.

Lash wrapped his arms around her. He savored the feel of her slick body draped over his own. His cock twitched. Her pussy answered in a tiny tremor. "Hmm, Nic..."

When he could manage it, he carried Teva to bed and crawled in beside her to cradle her close. Almost immediately, she dozed off. Her body was so warm pressed along his. So soft compared to the hard lines of his own.

Soon. He'd leave soon. Not yet, though. At the first rays of morning.

Occasionally through the hours, he woke Teva. She was like a flower. At his every touch, her petals opened up. He fingered her and tasted her all throughout the long night.

Finally, when he could wait no longer, he rolled her onto her stomach and pulled her hips up to stuff a pillow under them.

Teva moaned and wiggled.

Lash settled behind her ass to work his cock into her sticky hole. He poked and prodded like before, until she opened easily to accept his rigid length. Her pussy was as tight as he remembered. The sensation of filling her up would never be forgotten. How silky-soft her pussy was. How intense it would be when it milked his come.

Teva shifted in search of more cock.

With applied pressure, he forced her face down and her ass up more. His hands squeezed her ass as he watched the withdrawal and plunge in of his cock. Compulsion drove him to swivel his hips to screw his body in deep, and once it was buried, to dig around. She wiggled her ass. He wanted to know every caress of her pussy. Only this memory would hold him in the times to come. He'd memorize every angle of it.

She whimpered as her muscles clenched around him.

Lash gave it to her harder.

And then he fucked her faster.

Need tightened in his balls.

Soon, she panted with each thrust of his hard length. Lash grunted with each slap of his hips on her ass. The bed rocked with their movements. Brutally, he thrust. The faster and harder he drove his cock into her hole, the louder her cries sounded. He relished her every moan. Worked harder to make the fucking hotter.

She tensed under him. The climax that pulsed through her pussy provoked his own. "Teva." He groaned between his clenched teeth. His hips thrust with each jet of come.

He pulled away to kneel back. His chest heaved as he caught his breath. Reaching over, he removed the pillow from under her.

She spread her legs wide around him and plopped down on her belly. She no doubt already neared sleep again. But he had things to say, though all he wanted was another memory of her coming. He'd already been far too greedy. He had to go before he changed his mind. It would be so easy to stay as long as the lords allowed the reprieve. They could fuck all the time. He'd never get enough of Teva.

To stay would be selfish.

Chest aching, he slid to the edge of the bed to sit.

"Um, that was so great." Teva ran her hand across his lower back.

"Yes, it was." If only he could stay…He inhaled. No. It was time to go. "Teva…you are what makes…this so perfect." It was harder to breathe now then a few moments ago.

"Umhum..." She sighed. "I think it's you. You gonna get a drink of water?"

He had difficulty drawing a steady breath.

"Hurry up. We can do it again, but I'll do the work this time." The bed shifted, alerting him that she'd moved.

Lash's cock twitched. Instead of following the instinct to crawl back into bed, he reached up and removed the four-leaf clover she'd given him, which was a gift he had to return. The charm would never survive in Netherworld. And he'd cast his own spell over the charm. It'd help protect Teva now. He'd keep faith his prayer for her would be fate's will.

"Teva." He swallowed down his mounting misery over leaving. This was for the best. "Teva, I have to leave now."

"Huh? What?" The bed shifted once more. He forced himself to turn around. She now sat up. He wanted to reach out and caress a curl a final time. Touch her cheek just once before he left.

"I have to leave now."

Her eyes widened.

Go on, tell her the rest. Don't hold back. She has to believe. "I...I remember things."

"Oh, well, remembering is great." Her face looked pinched, as if she worked to hold back her emotions. "I guess this past you have has no place for me, huh?" The cords in her throat were tight. She reached for the blanket to hide behind.

How would he bear to say the truth? He couldn't bear to watch her hear the ugly words he must say.

"I love you, you know," she whispered.

Lash's eyes opened. "I...Teva, don't say that." *Please, Lord, I beg you—don't listen to her. She doesn't know what she says.* A tremble showed in his hands, so he balled them up. "Teva, I'm an evil man..."

"Nic, I can't believe that." She moved closer and folded her knees up to wrap her arms around herself. "Come on, don't think that way."

"I am." He swallowed. "And I've been lying to you from the beginning." Though the ache in his chest only tightened, his voice sounded firmer. "I'm pure evil. I was sent here to harm you."

"What?" Her lower lip quivered. She shifted slightly away.

The movement should have killed him. Too bad he was already dead, or it would have. He deserved the worst agony for what he was about to do to her. "The black magic you've spoken about, I'm part of it. I belong to that world."

"I don't understand..."

"I'm a condemned man."

"You've been to prison? Oh, Nic, everyone deserves a second chance."

"No, Teva, my kind does not." Lord forgive him, he couldn't say the words. "I must return home now."

She ran a hand through her hair and kept the blanket over her breasts. "What we shared was great." The quiver returned to her lips. The sight tore at his heart. "I believe in what we've shared."

The pain in his chest clenched. He forced himself to speak. To say the truth, no matter how he didn't want it to press past his lips. "The magic your aunt used is nothing compared to where I'm from..." He held her gaze. "Teva, I'm from Netherworld. Hell. My lords sent me here to ruin you."

She flashed him a weak smile. "Okay, look, if you've been having these kinds of memories, I think it's time we did take you to the hospital."

"I'm sorry for using you." He should have been stronger. Fucking her had been his most selfish act. "It was wrong of me."

She shook her head, curls bouncing. "Are you saying you believe you're a demon?"

"No. I'm a lost soul. I'm among the damned, who spend their eternity in Netherworld. The demons are my masters." His heart stalled at the fear now reflected in her gaze. "I'll never harm you. I swear it."

"We can get you some help..."

She still didn't believe him. He removed the bandage on his hand and held his palm out. "It's completely healed."

A frown puckered her mouth. The wheels turning in her mind showed in her gaze.

"You'll need this now." Lash passed her the charm, and when she wouldn't take it, he laid it on her pillow. "If you ever need anything, call for your guardian..." His mouth turned up. "...angel, Dion. He'll be able to protect you, if my spells ever fail." No doubt the lords would do their best to break his will back home.

He stood up.

She stared.

Three strides carried him to her dresser. He lifted the lid and withdrew a sharp, deadly-looking pair of scissors.

In the mirror, he caught her blue gaze. "Nic..." Her face paled as she clutched the blanket.

"I'll miss you forever." With those words, he forced the point into his chest cavity.

Crying out, Teva scrambled from the bed.

It was already too late. The sharp edge ripped into his heart. Lash applied even more force and pressed upwards. He winced at the feel of his life ebbing. With each pump of his heart, blood spilled out at a mad race.

He kept his eyes on Teva's movements. She rounded the end of the bed toward him. He could barely hear her talking now.

One erratic beat, which couldn't get his blood flowing.

A second pulse of his weak heart.

Teva's scream tore at his mind as a tiny, final beat worked within his chest before he fell.

⋘

Lash hit the ground of Netherworld with enough force to rattle his teeth. He groaned. He pushed up, only to be hauled by his hair. Ashton held him. "What a fool you are." The darken's face twisted in a sneer. "No pussy is worth angering our Prince." Ashton moved his face within an inch of Lash's. "He'll punish us all for your failure."

"She's worth any punishment we suffer. We're already condemned."

Ashton shoved him away and spat on his feet.

Yes, Teva was worth everything. For a brief moment, she'd loved him. In return, Lash would love her for all time. His knees weakened at the admission.

Ashton clamped a collar around his neck to drag him along. "Come on. Our Prince has ordered me to fetch you."

Lash would offer the darken no fight. His stomach rolled at the stench of the air. He'd never get used to the sickening smell. No one would. Just another punishment. Being allowed to get used to the ever-changing stink would be a reward.

Ashton jerked him over jagged rocks until they neared the

palace. Inside, the marble floor was cool to his raw feet. Lash had never been inside Netherworld's palace before. The rooms and halls shone magnificently with gold and jewels. The fact the Prince kept the palace so clean somehow amused Lash. Ashton didn't slow until they reached the Prince's chamber. A pair of darkens admitted them.

Their Prince, in human form, held court from his throne, where he inspected new female slaves. The large gold throne sat centered at the far wall. A beautiful, black-haired woman knelt at the Prince's feet. The woman was lean and lithe. She looked as bored as their Prince.

"Don't look at her," Ashton whispered from behind Lash's ear. "She's one of our lord's favorites." The darken pushed Lash to the center of the room.

Lash lowered his gaze to the Prince's feet. Their lord looked indifferent until his gaze settled on Lash. With one giant leap, the Prince landed directly in front of him. And roared. His fist hammered into the side of Lash's head to send him sprawling across the floor.

Ashton pulled him back to his feet by the chain.

"Be gone!" the Prince ordered, sending those in the room scrambling outside. Ashton dropped the chain, but the Prince stopped him. "Not you, slave."

Ashton trembled so hard that the chain rattled.

"Nor you, Sienna." The black-haired woman walked back to the throne steps. Her hand ran along the wall as she moved.

Lash had no more time to think before the Prince's claw cut open his middle to pull his intestines out.

He fell to his knees.

The Prince didn't let go of his insides. "Hook him to the wall."

Ashton dragged him away. Lash passed out, to revive to the snuffling and growls of Netherworld hounds. He bit his tongue to remain quiet as white-hot pain sent shockwaves throughout his body.

When next Lash awoke, he remained hooked to the wall by a chain. Ashton sat on the floor in the corner near him. The Prince sat on his throne. Sienna was impaled on their lord's cock. With her legs draped over that of their lord's, her legs were spread wider to allow them to see the Prince fucking her.

He glanced over. Ashton was sweating. Lash stayed still. He wanted to avoid another death at the muzzles of the dogs.

Sienna bounced up and down. Her juices flowed while the Prince lifted her higher and higher to slide her pussy back down to the base of his cock.

"Ashton, open your eyes." The Prince sounded far too gentle.

The darken looked at the couple.

"Do you want to see her take more of my cock?"

Sienna moaned, and her head rolled to the side.

"If it pleases you, my lord." Ashton's hands clenched.

The Prince's cock swelled huge. And then, it swelled larger still until it looked unbearable. Sienna did no more than groan as her hole repeatedly swallowed the monster cock.

The Prince fucked her in earnest then. Lash closed his eyes and rested while he had the chance. Sienna cried out, and his eyes opened to see their Prince sink fangs into the woman while he climaxed.

A shudder racked Lash's body. Demons often fed off of slaves to siphon off their emotions. Every emotion Sienna had had while fucking, the Prince had stolen.

When the couple caught their breaths, the Prince removed

her from his lap and stood. He positioned Sienna with her legs spread wide over the arms of his throne. "Ashton, come here and clean her cunt." He shoved several fingers into her hole. "I've got business to attend to." Removing the fingers, he offered them to Sienna to lick clean.

Across the room, Ashton dropped to his knees and buried his face, while Lash was jerked to his feet.

"Slave, let's go outside." The chain that held him to the wall disappeared while the collar remained. "I don't want to make another mess inside while I deal with you."

He wasn't even permitted to make it down the stairs before the Prince kicked him and broke several ribs.

Lash's wheeze alerted him to broken bones. A lung had possibly been punctured.

"You've defied me. You've placed a spell on Teva Gibson's home." The Prince's canines lengthened. "My forces can't get in." Fear clutched at his belly at the violence brewing in the Prince's red eyes. "And now you'll break your magic oath."

As if knowing Lash wouldn't break, at least not yet, the Prince whistled. Lash didn't hear sniffing, but the squeals and grunts of the wild boars. He closed his eyes; he wouldn't fold under any torture. Teva's soul depended on the protection spell.

For the second time that day, Lash suffered a slow, agonizing death as his innards were stretched out. This time unconsciousness was slower to claim him.

Reviving from death, he discovered the Prince in his true demon form. Lash rolled to keep from being trampled by a massive foot. Their lord tilted back his hairy face and roared. Netherworld shook. Lost souls wept from the show of temper.

Instead of making a run to hide, Lash ran up the beast's huge leg. He ran faster and just missed being torn into by a terrorizing claw. He moved up over a hip and along the Prince's hairy back. Here and there, he dove to miss the spiked tail sent to stab him. The beast screamed in fury every time it hurt itself. Lash was faster than the slow monster. He'd spent far too long training. He leaped onto its shoulder and climbed into its ear to miss another vicious claw sweep.

The Prince bellowed his rage. Netherworld rumbled in response. Slaves screamed and ran. Lash jumped out of the way of a single claw being driven into the ear canal.

"I'll never fail Teva." Now his heart beat only to protect her.

The beast shook its massive head.

Lash reached up to brace himself with his hands and feet, only to slip in wax. With a tilt of his head, Satan impaled Lash on a claw and withdrew him.

An eerie smile spread across the beast's face, as Lash hung suspended before its mouth. The next instant, his Prince swallowed him to begin the real torture.

☙

Teva was half-tempted to look for a hidden camera for a joke. But Nic wasn't that kind of guy. She squinted at where only moments before, Nic had stood. "Nic?" Weak-kneed, she sat on the bed as her heart continued to pound. Had she had some bizarre nightmare? "Nic?" Her voice rose to carry throughout the house. The sound vibrated in her head and chest. "Nic?"

Hands shaking, she yanked a t-shirt over her head before pulling some panties on. God, she was losing her mind. Her eyes burned. That had seemed like so much more than any dream, though. People didn't communicate in dreams, did they? Demons. Lost souls. A protection spell.

Knees knocking, she headed toward the bedroom door, only to stop at the sight that greeted her at the end of the bed.

Scissors lay on the floor beside the dresser. Her sewing scissors.

"Oh my God." Her head swam.

Okay, girl. You dropped them earlier and don't remember. People do not just disappear.

Teva searched her house from one end to the other. Nic wasn't there. Worst of all, his clothes remained. Back in her room, she picked up the clover charm. *You'll need this now*, Nic had said.

Oh God, what was going on? People did not disappear. They didn't.

Panicked, confused and scared, she looked around her room. What else had he said? Something about an angel? "Dion?" she whispered nervously. "Dion?" She was sure that was the name Nic had used.

"Boo" sounded behind her back.

She yelped and dropped the charm. "Oh, God." She swiveled around to meet the black gaze of a blond man. A very attractive man in a white t-shirt.

"Sorry about that." He didn't look the least bit apologetic. "Normally I'm summoned with screams of fear and never by my name. It was so much nicer this way, I couldn't resist."

"Are you real?" She blinked. The man remained. On a second look, she noted his broad shoulders and all the weapons he wore. Lots of weapons. She frowned. Would an angel wear weapons?

"Real?" A sneer spread across his handsome face. "We exist."

Of course, if one guy could disappear, logically, another

could appear. "We?" No matter how she tried to calm down, her heart continued to pound like a freight train over tracks.

"Fellowship of Light members."

"Angels?"

"Not many of us get wings. Only a legend or two." Dion's mouth twisted again. "We're more likely to be cast into Netherworld. Now what do you want? I'm sure you didn't get me here to say I prefer to see a woman in a thong."

"Huh? Oh." Quickly, she snatched up the sheet from the bed and sat down in the chair. Anger stirred to replace the churning fear. Dear God, Nic had disappeared. She hadn't imagined it. "Sit down. You're making me nervous towering over me."

He shrugged, but sat on the corner of the bed. "I don't get many calls for chit-chat either." He folded his arms. The sword which hung from his hip was huge and looked very real. As did the knives he wore. One rested at the waist of his black jeans. The other two were within his black boots. The handles rose up over the hem of his jeans.

"What are you?"

"We're known as sentinels. Gatekeepers." He placed his hands down on his thighs. "Demon hunters."

Now they were getting somewhere. "Demons?"

"Fierce furies. Poltergeists." Dion looked bored. "Familiars. Anything under Netherworld's rule."

"Great. I need you to go collect Nic. He's in real danger." A quiver set her lips to trembling. "I'm not sure what happened, but he disappeared."

The man smiled. It didn't reach his eyes. "Crazy mo-fo sent himself back to Netherworld, eh?" He shook his head. "Hadn't guessed he was a dumbass."

Teva's back stiffened.

I'll miss you forever. Oh God, Nic had loved her and had left her to protect her and this...this asshole... "I want you to help Nic."

"No can do. He's history. Forget about him." He wiped his hands along his thighs. "I can make you forget him. With a brush of my psyche, you'll not remember a thing about his stay with you."

She gasped and stood up. "Don't you dare."

"Hey." He raised his hands. "Only a suggestion."

"If you don't have the balls or the know-how to help me find him, who does?" Anger blazed in her heart. She wanted Nic back.

"Look." Dion stood up. Pinched his nose and mumbled something under his breath. "Only a dumbass goes into Netherworld. Your *lover* has been sentenced to an eternity in Hell."

"Nic doesn't deserve to be there." The fear returned to beat a rapid pace in her heart. She hated to think of Nic there. "He's a good guy."

He snorted. "You tell me what condemned man doesn't feel that way. Look, you've got the hots for him. You'll get over it. A couple of weeks, you'll meet someone new to make..."

She glared.

He shrugged. "Was the sex the best of your life? Come on, lady. He's been in Netherworld for eons. He probably didn't let you out of bed."

"Oh...you..." Teva wanted to slap him. Nic was a keeper. She'd repeatedly thrown herself at him sexually, and he'd fought the attraction. Now she had no doubt Nic had wanted her just as much, just as badly, as she'd wanted him. He'd finally caved. Her heart ached when the truth hit. He'd made love to her to hold on to the memory. Tears burned her throat. Oh God, how was she going to help Nic? "Who has the power to help him?"

Dion folded his arms across his chest. "Besides our Lord?"

"Yes." Her teeth clenched as she clutched the sheet to keep her body hidden.

"A fate. Or an archangel."

Dear God, a fate or an archangel? How did someone plead a case to such power? "How do I speak to one of them?"

"You can't. A fate can never be contacted, and well, archangels only intercede when they want to. " He smiled. "As I said, I'm a gatekeeper. We go between the living and the Afterlife."

"And you won't help me?"

"Not a chance."

Fine. She'd find another way. "Dion?"

"What?"

"You don't deserve your wings." She lifted her chin.

He glared, clapped his hands and disappeared in a flash.

Good riddance. She didn't need his help. She'd find another way to help Nic all on her own. Her mom's spells would be a good starting point.

Chapter Eighteen

Teva's head hurt. She closed the spell book with a slap. Her mom had spells to dispel a lesser demon, a demon horde, a familiar, and a greater demon, but, not a single one to call forth one. How much difference could there be in a lesser and a greater demon?

Far too much time had been spent combing through the pages. She'd gotten caught up in exploring the elemental spells and those concerning illusions. So fascinating. Now she knew how her dad had done those magic tricks. Camouflage was a powerful tool. How easy it was to trick the human eye or prey in the wild.

She shivered as fine hairs on her forearms stood up on end. There had also been spells to destroy the undead. The spells hadn't explained what exactly undead meant. She released a calming breath and climbed to her feet.

Since her mom's spells hadn't panned out, she moved on to plan B. Jenna's cousin. It took only a couple minutes to perform an online search for Ally's shop.

No more time to waste. She headed into New Orleans. She had to locate someone who had the know-how to help. She climbed into the driver's seat and tears filled her eyes. Nic had driven last. Reaching down between her legs, she grasped the lever and shifted the seat forward. She had to move up so she could reach the pedals.

Black Sabbath's *Dehumanizer* album kept her company as scenery slipped by.

The gas light chimed, alerting her that soon she'd be pushing. As soon as possible, she pulled into a local diner and gas station.

"Fill up?" Old Bobby Hanes leaned over by her window.

She dug into her purse. "Twenty, please." How long had the guy worked here? She could remember him pumping her parents' gas when she was a child.

"You bet."

Once the jeep was fueled, she went through the motions. "Thanks, Bobby." He took the money with a dirty hand, and she parked to run inside for a soda to go.

The compact store used half its small space to hold quick-stop items. The other half was the diner with little white tables and red chairs. The fluorescent lights made it appear bright.

Before she reached the counter, Jackson waved her over.

Bottle in hand, she made her way over to the group.

Jackson stood and tipped his baseball cap. The group of men were all in their seventies and eighties. She'd seen the cronies in the diner many times. "Hey." She waved to everyone.

The others greeted her. One of the men didn't wear his false teeth. It was obvious when he smiled.

Jackson excused himself. "I'll walk you out. I got some information."

Shoulders slumped, she paid for her drink. Jackson held the door for her, and they walked in silence to the edge of the old building. Teva had no desire to tell the old guy Nic was gone.

"The young fella tell you I stopped by?"

"Yeah. Thanks for your help. It means a lot." God, let her need his help getting Nic some ID.

The old guy spit tobacco juice.

Teva curled her nose. She'd never been able to figure out the appeal of chew. Yuck.

"Did he mention a peculiar smell at your place?"

Dryness engulfed her mouth. She worked her tongue around nervously. "Yeah, he might have."

"Well, it hit me the other night..." He spat again. "Way back in '84, I had the worst case of my career."

She nodded.

"Real mess." He shook his head as if remembering. "FBI got involved. A satanic cult had been holding gatherings...orgies, ritual killings..." His nose curled above his beard. "And this god-awful scent. The thing is, it wasn't a bad smell on its own...it's just...I'll never forget it."

"Um, any arrests in the case?"

"Not a one. In fact, the woman who'd contacted us wound up dead. Real shame, too. Nice lady." He braced his palm on the wall. "The group hightailed it out of these parts. Truth is, even now the satanic cult is the most secretive of societies. Law enforcement agencies have little on them."

After today, she could see how easy that could be. So far, she'd witnessed two people disappear. The powers of darkness wouldn't have trouble protecting their supporters.

"Easier to track a terrorist cell." Jackson pushed off from the building. "Real shame. Anyway, you be careful out there. And give that husband of yours a slap on the back for me." He tipped his hat and shuffled away.

Releasing a long breath, she went along with his memory.

Over the past year or two, he'd often thought she was her mom.

Once in New Orleans, she parked and walked the few blocks to Ally Cease's shop. Yummy scents teased her stomach into rumbling. Restaurants, bars, and gift shops dotted every street. The place wasn't hard to find. Not only was she fond of the grand old city, but she was completely familiar with its streets. The city had changed so much since the natural disaster. Many of residents had relocated, even those in the French Quarter.

Thankfully, tourism had picked up.

Carefully, she stepped up into the dark interior. The clerk immediately offered a welcome.

"Hi. I'm looking for Ally Cease."

"That's me. What can I do for you?" She continued to sort some beads.

"Oh, great." She stepped across the wood floor to the high counter. "I knew Jenna..."

The woman's black eyes pinned her.

"She told me to contact you."

"Ah, yes, Jenna called me only moments before she died."

Teva winced with pain. "I'm so sorry about her passing."

"We live. We die. Not much any of us can do to change those facts."

She nodded. "I'm hoping you could help me with a spell..."

"Ah, yes, Jenna mentioned..."

"Well, you see, circumstances have changed...I need a spell to summon a demon."

The woman's black eyes narrowed in suspicion and anger. She reached down underneath her counter and pulled out some sort of bag. She shook it violently in Teva's face. "Get out!"

Staring at the wild-eyed woman, she backed away.

Ally muttered something Teva didn't understand as she advanced around the counter.

Teva turned and nearly fell off the shop's step in her haste.

"Don't you ever enter my shop again, and keep your evilness away from the rest of my family."

"No, you don't understand..." She trailed off as the woman continued to mutter and shake her rattle in Teva's direction.

People stopped to gawk.

Teva's heart pounded at the hate the woman spewed at her. After it didn't let up, she turned and ran. She didn't stop until she reached Jackson Square, where she collapsed on a bench. Oh God, the woman had scared her.

Panting, she berated herself. She hadn't considered Jenna would've had time to contact Ally. And never would she have thought Ally would consider her evil.

She raked her hair away from her face.

This left one option.

Clarisse.

૭ૐ

Bile rose in Lash's throat. Physically ill, he couldn't take his eyes from the big screen, which showed him and the others Teva's every move.

What, in all that was holy, was she thinking? She wanted to call forth a demon? A fucking demon. The thought of her doing something so horrid should bring forth another death for him. Only her actions didn't, he continued to exist. His heart thundered in concern for Teva. The fear for her tormented him. He supposed that's why the demons permitted him to watch.

How would he ever protect her, if she succeeded?

Abruptly, he dropped to the ground to crumple in a heap. His shoulders and arms throbbed a slow ache. They'd gone numb from hanging too long. Blood returned to his limbs, and he rubbed to rush the flow along.

Asmodeus stepped behind their Prince and whispered something for his ears only. Surely the lord of lust encouraged the Prince to commit more sins of the flesh.

Sienna slept with her hand and face on their lord's right foot while he sat in his throne. The slave had slept for hours as the lords were entertained by Teva's mission. The Prince's stillness had surprised him. Lash had never known of a slave to be permitted rest in Netherworld. What would become of the woman once the Prince grew bored of her?

The screen caught his attention once more. Teva climbed back into her jeep. Sienna's problems didn't matter. He had plenty of his own.

Teva do not do this. I beg you.

On screen, Teva's blue eyes widened, and she looked around.

Lash continued to look on. Had she heard him? He recalled what the guardian had said about his people. How they'd possessed powerful psyches. He pushed with his mind.

"Teva, I beg you. Leave it be. Go on with your life."

This time, on screen Teva turned in her seat to look around. *Lord, she can hear me.*

"Nic?" She sounded from the screen's speakers.

All eyes turned toward him. Fear ignited in his guts when the Prince's eyes blazed. Had Lash been caught in his latest attempt to help Teva? Did the Prince remember his people's psychic abilities?

Instead of exploding in anger, the Prince controlled himself.

Teva turned her music on and drove onward.

"Ashton?" Satan motioned to the darken hanging back. "Take Sienna to my bedchamber and see she's bathed and fed a meal." Gently, the Prince reached down to urge the slave to wake. "Up, Sienna. I'll join you later."

She was disoriented, but given no time to protest before Ashton grasped her hand to lead her away. The Prince's hungry eyes followed the sway of her ass until she was out of sight. Only then did he turn his mounting fury on Lash. "Nicodemus, you are reaching the end of my patience."

Eyes lowered, Lash kept his fists clenched, waiting for the first blow.

"And now you try to play mind games? Have you already forgotten where the ability got your ancestors?"

He had forgotten a great many things about his previous life. The reminder set the memories in motion. The Olympians had despised his people. Had believed them frightful in their ability to use their minds. To see the future. The Olympians had done everything within their immense power to make his people's lives miserable. And when the oracles hadn't forecast what the Olympians had wanted to hear, they'd been cursed to live as giants and be feared by all.

That had been when his people's real struggle had begun.

All his people had wanted was to live free of the strict tyranny. Their hate-filled desire and warring to exterminate the Olympians had cost them greatly. Reality had been harsh when many of his race wound up toiling beside the Olympians for all eternity.

"Slave, I'll give you but one more chance." The Prince's eyes blazed blood red. "Break the magic oath and let my followers inside the woman's home."

Lash inhaled a deep breath, only to gag on the putrid scent. "Never." He'd do everything in his power to protect Teva.

"So be it." His lord turned into a raging bull and attacked him. He was gored and viciously stomped until they reached the outer bank of a river. Lash suffered a quick death when a hoof crushed his skull.

He revived to suck in freezing air. Satan changed to his human self.

The pit of Netherworld. His Prince had brought him to the bank of the Cocytus River. Already, the bone-chilling cold slowed his blood.

"A fitting place for a traitor among my brood." His lord made yet another transformation to his demon soul. Lash was kicked to the middle of the frozen river. He slid belly first until he hit a half-hidden boulder. He grunted when his shoulder was dislocated on impact. The ice shattered underneath his weight to engulf him. Lash fought to the surface. He bobbed up. The river froze as Satan's breath rushed across to the other bank.

Icy pain crawled along his body to set his teeth chattering.

His lord took flight with gigantic wings to circulate more power and wind over the river.

Numbness from the cold was slow to penetrate his covered body. His eyes froze open while his eyelashes broke off in the fierce wind.

"Break the magic oath, and I'll break the ice to set you free." The monster's wings kicked up an ice blizzard.

Lash could barely breathe. *"Never."* He pushed back into the Prince's mind.

In a fit of temper, the dark lord broke his neck. Lash revived from another death to discover the Prince had left him alone in his icy tomb. The act of continually freezing sparked endless agony. Slowly, his body froze solid to crack into pieces, but the pain was no worse than to burn to death or be drawn and quartered.

"*Teva, allow the protection spell to keep you safe. I beg you.*"

The Prince's admittance that his spell was strong enough warmed his heart. If Teva would only allow it to last.

☙

Teva wiped her eyes yet again. She'd been crying most of the evening. Ever since she'd begun to hear Nic's voice. Repeatedly, he asked her to leave well enough alone.

Dear God, she couldn't. She loved him and couldn't bear to have him live in Hell.

The guy she'd known didn't deserve that kind of eternity. And, after what she'd seen in her dreams, many deserved a second chance at redemption. So she'd called Clarisse and asked her to make a stop out here. The clock chimed the hour, and Teva moved to wait out on the porch.

Clarisse was only a few minutes late, but it was late enough for Teva to worry the woman wouldn't show.

She stood as the car entered her empty lane. A frown creased her forehead when Clarisse could pull no further than the bonfire pit near the driveway. She bet the protective block was a full circle around her house. This proved two things. One, Nic had serious willpower. And two, Clarisse did mean her harm.

Once she pushed her hair back from her face, she walked out to the firepit to get closer. "Hello, Clarisse," she greeted her aunt as the woman climbed out of her car. Clarisse looked older today, less elegant.

"Hello, dear. Aren't you going to invite me in?" Malice swam in her gaze.

Teva shook her head. "Nope." She toyed with the four-leaf clover, which now hung around her neck. "It's nice weather." No way did she want Clarisse in her home. Still, she needed her help. "No more games, Clarisse. I know you've tried to do me harm." And although she wanted to know why, she wanted to save Nic more.

The older woman's eyes widened in false shock. Teva wanted to roll her eyes and slap the woman at once. "If you give me a spell, I'll forgive you."

"And you believe I'd want your forgiveness?" Clarisse walked along the outside of the imaginary protective fence until she stood nearer to Teva.

"Everyone needs forgiveness at one time or another."

"What kind of spell?"

"One I'm sure you've used before."

Clarisse's mouth pursed.

"I need to call forth a demon."

"Ah. A demon?' Her aunt flashed an ugly smile." Which one, dear?"

"You tell me, aunt. You're the one practiced in black magic."

"I might be able to offer a suggestion or two. There are several demons quite willing to make bargains"

"Teva, I beg you, do not do this thing."

"Oh, God, Nic. I love you so much. Can you hear me?" Teva's knees knocked. *"Please hear me."*

"Yes."

Her heart hammered. *Thank you, God.* She swallowed. *"Nic,*

I love you so much."

"If that is true, then listen to my wish. Leave this be and go on with your life."

Nic didn't have to say it. She knew in her soul that he loved her in return. Not only loved her, but was in love with her. She focused on her aunt. "I need to summon one demon who is both powerful and can be bought." She prayed that even among demons, there were a few noble beings. In this case, she needed an untrustworthy being. Hopefully, one her aunt had bargained with before.

"Fine. Asmodeus will suit."

Again, Teva offered up a silent prayer. She'd given herself a crash course on demons at the library on the way home. The name was one she recognized. "Is that his ring you wear?"

Clarisse admired the heavy jewel, which circled her ring finger. She smiled. "Repeat after me."

Teva's mouth dried out, yet she managed to nod.

"'Magic forces dark and light."

"Magic forces dark and light." Teva mouthed the words without a shred of self will.

"Transcend through space and light."

"Transcend through space and light." Again Teva mimicked her aunt without a smidgeon of energy.

"Be he far, or be he near. Bring me the demon Asmodeus here." Clarisse's eyes widened at the feel of the Earth trembling under their feet. "No! It's not supposed to be like this!"

Her aunt had invited a demon to Earth outside the protective spell. Clarisse had rushed in her greed and hate, allowing Teva to trick her. "No!"

Though Teva had hoped the trap would work, she didn't get a rush of happiness at the panic in her aunt's eyes. After her flight from Ally's shop, Teva had tried to think of a better plan. While she wanted to help Nic, she also didn't want to sacrifice herself until she'd used up every other option.

Intuition told her Nic now suffered for his protective magic. She loved him more for his sacrifice. So she needed the demon outside her safety zone. She also wanted to know why Clarisse had tried to harm her.

Before her now stood a three-headed creature. The image didn't last. In a blink, the monster transformed to a handsome man with the body and face of an Adonis.

Clarisse's moment of weakness was gone. The woman reached out and grasped the man's engorging cock to stroke him to his full length.

Asmodeus smirked. "What do you think of your aunt's beauty, Teva?" With a wave of his hand, her aunt's clothes vanished. Clarisse's body had held up as well as her face over the decades.

Stomach churning, Teva stared. Had the demon helped her aunt stay young? Was a spell strong enough to hold off destiny? And what price had her aunt paid?

"Asmodeus, I have missed you." Clarisse pulled the demon's face down to plant a kiss on his mouth. She continued to pump his cock.

Now *this*, she hadn't planned on. Teva looked away only to glance back at her aunt's cry. Worry clutched her heart. The demon dragged Clarisse by the hair.

Teva took a step forward.

"No. It is a trap like the way you trapped her. Asmodeus lords over lust. Clarisse is more than willing."

Nic was probably right. Her aunt wasn't fighting to escape.

Asmodeus laid Clarisse back onto the hood of her car and

brought her legs up. He placed her aunt's ankles over his shoulders.

From the corner of her eye, a flash caught her attention. Another demon had appeared, followed by another and another and yet more.

Dear God...

With a shaking hand, she withdrew a spell from her pocket. She'd copied a vanishing spell, just in case things went bad. Too bad the spell wasn't meant to get rid of an army of demons. Still more poured out of the hole her aunt had somehow opened. One after another ugly creature joined its companions to dance wildly around her yard.

"*Teva, get in the house.*" Nic sounded on edge.

She glanced in Clarisse's direction.

"*Go! There's another protective spell within your home.*"

Terrified, she turned and ran. A demon she'd expected to take on. An army, she had not.

Chapter Nineteen

Netherworld forever remained a place of despair, chaos, and pain. Yet never had Lash been so wretchedly assaulted by turmoil. After suffering three deaths from the frigid cold, he'd been left alone imprisoned in the water. Another viewing screen had been presented for Lash. Tormented, he'd watched Teva put her ludicrous plan into action. He wanted to shake her for her foolishness. All the while, he wanted to protect her from those out to do her harm.

How could she not know the danger she risked? Anger boiled hot in his veins. *Lord, I beg you, don't allow the darkness to claim Teva.* He prayed to the Lord of the Afterlife to save Teva.

She deserved so much more than Netherworld.

On screen, Teva ran toward her home as a dozen more demons erupted through the hole opened by Clarisse. Lash strained against the ice and freezing water that imprisoned him. He fought like a maniac to break free of his tomb, to no avail.

Left with no recourse, he reached out with his mind. *"Teva, call for Dion."*

She snorted, but when the fervent prayers brushed his mind, he backed away.

Next he called on two of his people he'd heard legends of. The giants Antaeus and Ephialtes. *"I beg you, cousins, to help break the ice which surrounds me."*

"Why should we help you? It would only bring grief down on our heads." Antaeus sounded clearly in his mind.

Lash grunted. How had he forgotten the power of their minds? Antaeus hadn't forgotten the ability.

Antaeus had been rumored to carry lost souls to Cocytus. The giant had to be familiar with this area of Netherworld. Ephialtes, the giant son of Poseidon, surely knew how to manipulate water by magic. He could think of no two others in the position to help his cause. He had to be free to make a run for Netherworld's gates. Perhaps those of light and goodness couldn't hear his prayers from the bowels of Netherworld. He didn't want to think they ignored Teva's danger.

Ephialtes surprised him by coming to his aid. The giant shook the ground as he moved to the edge of the water. "I know this is going to get me some hard labor, but it'll make my father proud." Ephialtes threw back his head and laughed from his belly. The mountains rumbled. "Anything to piss *our lord* off." The giant leaned down and jabbed the river, cracking it in the middle. "This is going to kill you..."

The rest went unsaid. Another death was simply another death to his kind.

Ephialtes jabbed again and again before the ice shattered enough to where Lash could be freed. Lash came to on the other side of the river.

"Go north, cousin." Antaeus's mind spoke. *"You have to reach the center of Netherworld. There will be a stream of sweet water. You'll never reach Purgatory before the winged demons hunt you. But maybe it's far enough to reach those you seek?"*

Purgatory. Where Dion lived. There would be more sentinels there to help save Teva. "Have you ever heard of one reaching Purgatory?"

"No, but there's a first time for everything. Now go. The

hounds have already been sent out."

On screen, Teva had her back against the door with her eyes screwed shut as she prayed. *"Dear Lord, send Dion to her aid."*

In the distance, Lash could hear the growls and barks of the hungry beasts. He bolted north to the center of Netherworld. Lash didn't fool himself as he ran. The Prince toyed with him. It was only a matter of time before the winged demons were sent to join the hunt.

His bare feet pounded across the rugged, cold ground as one word pulsed with every beat of his heart. *Justice.* The word had been used by Dion. Justice was what Lash wanted most for Teva. She didn't deserve what she now dealt with. A demon horde against one lone human. What was just in that action?

Half-tempted to drop to his knees in prayer, Lash ran on, mile after mile. He had to get as close to Purgatory as possible to make sure he could be heard. *Dear Lord, let justice be served this day. Protect Teva.*

Mid-step, Lash's feet left the ground. Warmth spread through his body as he teleported, not with violent force, but with care and gentleness.

The roar of the Prince followed him, along with demons in flight.

03

Lash appeared as Dion flashed into Teva's living room. With a gasp, she threw her arms around Lash's neck. He allowed himself only a moment to enjoy her embrace.

A look of disgust spread across Dion's face after the man looked outside. "Have you seen the party out there?"

Teva squeaked. "Oh my God, Clarisse..."

"Clarisse, my ass." Dion folded his arms. "You had *something* to do with this."

Lash growled.

Teva placed her hand on his chest. "Well, yeah, but I meant to save Nic."

Dion met his eyes. "Sword or daggers?"

While Lash had once wielded a sword, it had been far too long since he'd been sentenced to Netherworld. "Daggers." Killing would be easier up close and personal.

Dion tossed him two. He caught them by their handles. Dion turned away, but not before Lash noted the new emotion which stirred within their black depths of his eyes. The man feared the demons.

Lash frowned. "Dion, what happens if they kill you instead?"

Dion glanced back as he pulled the door open. "Go straight to Hell. Do not pass go." Then the guardian walked outside to confront his enemies.

Teva moaned. "I can't believe this is happening."

Lash kissed her on the temple. All that mattered was keeping her safe. The sentinel had known that, too. That's why the man had shown up. "Keep the door locked. No one comes inside."

She nodded, and he followed Dion outside. The guardian had already crossed the protective boundary. His sword flashed a white light every time it impaled a demon. The creatures disappeared with a scream and a flurry of dust.

Lash positioned himself to protect Dion's back. On a prayer of forgiveness, he jabbed out at a leaping demon. The dagger thrust through the creature's heart. Shrieking, the being disappeared. Time after time, Lash struck a demon to watch it disappear. Still, the number never grew smaller. He and Dion were clearly outnumbered.

Dion fought with the skill and inexhaustible energy of a seasoned warrior. Heads rolled. Limbs were severed. Bellies ripped open. All from the steel of the sentinel's swinging sword.

Lash caught one demon up on his dagger, barely noticing the claws that raked down his chest.

Teva rushed outside, breaking his concentration. He bumped Dion's back when a demon rammed him. Lash shoved the dagger home, sending the creature back to Netherworld.

Teva cried louder as she chanted.

"What is she doing?" Lash asked himself as much as Dion.

"No clue. I've never understood humans, let alone the females." Dion panted between arcs of his sword.

In between thrusts of the daggers, Lash tried to make out Teva's words. Her words kept repeating. She must be trying to cast a spell.

Dear Lord, get her back inside. He shoved the dagger through the throat of a two-headed demon. It poofed into dust, only to reveal another circling replacement.

Clarisse left her position in Asmodeus's lap to approach Teva. She stopped at the protective border.

"Don't pay the bitch any mind. Keep fighting." Dion killed another creature.

"Teva, listen to me. To stop this madness, all you have to do is cross over to me." Clarisse beckoned to Teva with her arms. "Your lover will be saved."

Teva took a step forward.

Lash's heart caught. "She lies!" He stabbed a demon, then another. Desperate need weakened his knees. He wanted to go to Teva, but he dared not leave Dion's back. Too many demons remained. He refused to see the guardian reside in Netherworld because of them. "I cannot be saved." Lash stabbed one demon, only to jab another. With a cloud of dust, they disappeared.

Dion's sword clanked on shell as the greater demons replaced the lesser ones. With the advantage of the daggers, Lash slid the sharp ends under the shells and blinked to see them poof. Dion grunted as a claw got him. Lash moved closer once more. Now the creatures worked hard to get to Dion on their right and left flanks.

"Teva, dear, you don't want to see this man face the same fate your lover once faced, do you?'

"As if." Dion sneered. "Don't listen to the bitch."

Asmodeus, the lord of lust, leapt from the hood of the car. He grabbed a nearby demon and hurled it into the protective boundary. Electrified, the creature shrieked and disappeared. "Enough. I've been promised a soul. I don't care whose I take with me this night." The demon lord tossed one after another lesser demon into the protective spell in an attempt to weaken the hold.

"Promised a soul?" Lash stabbed out at an approaching monster.

"The bitch must have bargained for Teva's soul." Dion's sword clanked on more shell.

Fury erupted from Lash. "How dare she?" How dare anyone forfeit another's fate?

"It happens regularly," Dion gritted through his teeth as he turned another night creature to dust.

With growing speed, Asmodeus threw his horde against the spell's border. Lash's heart hammered in his chest. The lord now focused on a center spot. Would the spell continue to hold?

Asmodeus turned and pointed at Lash. "Focus on him. I only need a second of weakness to get through."

The demons attacked him as one. Dion cursed and turned his back. He came around to fight the demons off Lash.

"No." His heart caught at the fear on Teva's face. "Stay to my back."

Dion ignored him.

From the corner of his eye, he saw Clarisse join the demon lord's power with magic of her own. She sent fireballs in-between the hurled demons.

Dear Lord, I beg you, protect them. If I had a soul to give, I'd give it for them. If I could die but one more time…I would for them.

Dion grunted as if in pain. Lash didn't dare risk to see if the man had been injured.

A bright light burst forth, opening up the night sky. Lash dropped the daggers as a glowing being floated to Earth. "Vile wind that blows. No longer may you dwell here among the light. Death returns you to Netherworld with this magic." What could only be an angel spread his arms wide and lifted his head to the heavens. Electricity crackled above them.

Asmodeus and the other demons vanished in a heavy cloud of dust.

Clarisse screamed and tried to hide her nakedness. She wasn't the woman she'd been when she'd arrived. Now, instead of a beautiful middle-aged woman, hunched an old hag. Clarisse continue to wail as she slowly hobbled to her car.

Lash fought to catch his breath.

Dion dropped to his knees while the old woman sped away and out of sight. Teva ran to Lash's side.

"Justice has been served. Teva Gibson, you will know no

more demons." The glowing being floated over and placed a warm hand on Lash's shoulder. "With this touch, I heal Nicodemus. He has proven redemption and in doing so, has earned salvation."

His throat worked. Could it possibly be?

"You've been given a second chance to live on Earth." The powerful being squeezed Lash's shoulder one time and released him. The man stepped back. "And you, Dion..."

Placing his sword in its sheath, the guardian smiled. "Earned my wings." He stood.

The angel sighed. "No. But, you have earned a day of rest."

"Beggars can't be choosers." Dion picked up his daggers to hide them away. On a clap, the guardian disappeared.

"My aunt?" Teva whispered. "What will happen to her?"

"Clarisse made a bargain with a demon. It's only a matter of time before she'll pay the price." The angel shook his head sadly. "She sought to remain young and beautiful forever. Though she's committed many sins, her real crime was bargaining with something that didn't belong to her." He took Teva's chin in his palm. "There's nothing that can be done to save her now. Her fate has been sealed. Her eternity won't be the pretty one she'd hoped."

Lash knelt. "Thank you." He'd been given the greatest of gifts.

"Oh, don't thank me. I'm only a messenger." Then he too vanished.

☙

Warm water sprayed his body. Teva pressed up along his back. Her soapy hands lathered his skin in their wake. The shower soothed him as much as Teva's touch aroused his senses. His cock stood straight out from his body.

A second chance at life. A chance to have Teva at his side.

"Um...I don't think I can get you any cleaner." She placed kisses along his back. "In fact, I think it's time we got a little bit dirty."

Need pulsed in his cock. A need to show her how much she meant to him. The words were there on the tip of his tongue, but to show her would so much more intense. So much more pleasurable.

"Um, dirty?"

Her hand drifted lower to clasp his cock. She stroked. "Oh, yes. I want to get very sticky." Firm fingers ran up and down his length until the tingle in his balls got to be too much for him.

Gently, he removed her hand and kissed her palm. Lash turned around to have her breasts press into his chest. Her nipples teased him with their tautness.

Nostrils flaring, he leaned down. He took first the right treasure into his mouth and then the left. She gasped each time a nipple slid from his suctioning lips. Her hips jerked, and he lowered to his knees. Teva grabbed the towel bar as he lifted a leg to prop her foot on the tub.

Lash's tongue darted out to lave her slit before toying with her clit.

"Oh, Nic." She moaned. "Oh God, don't play now."

So he didn't. He sucked the little bundle of nerves into his mouth and shoved two fingers into her hot, tight hole. His fingers thrust a mad pace while his lips sucked hard to keep the pressure steady.

The tension in her body grew, alerting him climax neared. He sucked harder. Teva cried out as her hips arched. Silken pussy walls convulsed around his fingers until her body finally relaxed.

He stood and licked his fingers. Then he kissed her mouth. Her free arm slid around his neck. He lifted her leg higher to work it over his hip.

He lowered only briefly to bring the tip of his cock to her pussy. He prodded the hole to accept his rigid length.

She moaned as he shoved his cock in deeper. Needing to be even further in, he straightened to drive his cock hard into her slick depths. Her pussy was hot and grasping.

Lash grabbed her ass to lift her higher. He wanted to be planted inside her to his balls.

Her breath rushed into his ear, and she wrapped both arms around him. Their bodies were hot and wet as they slid along one another.

Teva brought her other leg up to wrap it around his other hip. One of his hands braced them against the wall as his other gripped her ass.

Balls-deep, he groaned and flexed his ass.

She whimpered, her pussy sucking at his cock. "I love you so much, Nic."

His knees nearly buckled. "Teva." He swallowed. "Ah, Teva." His balls drew up. He pumped his hips to send his cock violently into her hole. Her pussy sucked at his cock with every stroke.

"I love you, Nic." She panted along with each beat of his heart. "I love you. I love you."

The trembling shook his body. Still, he fucked her hard. Deep. He thrust into her softness until she could do no more than cling to him.

The climax which claimed her drove him over the edge. Hot

come burst out to fill her up. Tight pussy muscles milked him to his last drop.

Teva moaned and slid from his body. Noting the trembling in her legs, he turned the water off and grabbed a towel. He wrapped it around her quivering body. He stepped out first and picked her up. She rested her head upon his shoulder.

In her bedroom, he dried her off and tucked her under the blanket. As soon as he climbed in beside her, she kissed him on the lips. "I love you, Nic."

"Teva, I..."

She kissed him again. "Have you looked in a mirror yet?"

He shook his head.

"You have the most gorgeous bright blue eyes. But I think I'm going to miss the black ones." He'd been given back his original eye color. His brother had had that shade, too.

"Teva..."

"The mark is gone from your back."

He reached over his shoulder and could no longer feel the raised brand. "I..."

She kissed him before he could say the needed words. Her sweet tongue played with his to leave him breathing hard.

"Um...Nic...I hate to bring this up now..."

His chest constricted at the look in her eyes.

"I think we may want to practice safe sex. I mean, I know I didn't give it a thought before. Before everything." A flush spread across her cheeks. "I just wasn't thinking clearly."

"Safe sex."

"Um...You know when you shoot your come inside me..."

He lifted up on an elbow. "You don't want me to..."

"Oh." She smiled. "I want you to. Believe me, I want you

to." She kissed his mouth. "But I don't want to trap you in any way."

"Trap me?" What foolishness. He smiled and rolled over on top of her soft curves. He slid his cock along her slick pussy until it thickened. He shoved it back into her hole with little prodding.

She gasped. "Oh."

"I love you." He pushed forward with a thrust of his hips.

"Hmm." Her hands buried in his hair to bring his lips closer. "I love you more, Nic Lash."

Lowering his head, he brushed his lips across her full mouth. He planned to prove her wrong. And thankfully, he had a lifetime to prove the depth of his love.

About the Author

Melissa Lopez writes for herself. She creates her worlds for her characters. She is an author of fantasy, contemporary, dark urban fantasy, futuristic, historical, paranormal, suspense, and erotic romance.

To learn more about Melissa Lopez, please visit www.melissa-lopez.com. Send an email to Melissa at Melissa@melissa-lopez.com or join her Yahoo! group to join in the fun with other readers as well as Melissa! http://groups.yahoo.com/group/melissalopez.

Take a walkabout on the wild side.

Boomerang Love
© *2008 Melissa Lopez*

When you toss a boomerang, you know it will come back. But all bets are off when it's a lover you've let go.

Cohen Thorn and Hayleigh Davenport shared one night of wild sex neither of them can forget, then went their separate ways half a world apart. But now Hayleigh's back in Australia for one more weekend of passion. If she can't get this Outback rancher out of her system once and for all, she'll at least have memories to last a lifetime.

They've only got three days to steam up Sydney and the Outback, but in the place known as Never-Never, anything can happen. Soon they realize there's a powerful force drawing them together.

Is it simple lust, or lasting love?

Available now in ebook from Samhain Publishing.

Quinn excels at slaying demons. But betrayal is the one demon she never saw coming.

Stripped Away
© 2008 Sydney Somers

Nothing gives Quinn a rush like hunting and vanquishing the very demons that changed her life. But lately something is off. Way off. Nightmares she can't explain, irrational fears surfacing at the most unexpected moments. And when her twin sister vanishes, Quinn's world starts to come apart at the seams.

Since becoming an agent for the Shadow Destroyers, Braxton has excelled at playing by the rules. Until, in a moment of weakness, he let his common sense desert him for one night in Quinn's arms. A night she doesn't remember. For weeks he's kept their relationship strictly professional, but seeing Quinn so edgy and lost puts his telepathic abilities—and his restraint—to the test.

As the search for her sister intensifies and everything Quinn thought she knew comes into question, Braxton seems to be the one true thing she can hold onto. Until she discovers he's been keeping a very big secret of his own.

One that may destroy her trust just when she needs him the most.

Available now in ebook and print from Samhain Publishing.

GREAT CHEAP FUN

Discover eBooks!

THE FASTEST WAY TO GET THE HOTTEST NAMES

Get your favorite authors on your favorite reader, long before they're out in print! Ebooks from Samhain go wherever you go, and work with whatever you carry—Palm, PDF, Mobi, and more.

Samhain Publishing Ltd

WWW.SAMHAINPUBLISHING.COM

Printed in the United States
140321LV00005B/2/P